The Clouds Are Big With Mercy

Fred Urquhart

The Clouds Are Big with Mercy

Fred Urquhart

WITH AN INTRODUCTION BY
ISOBEL MURRAY

Kennedy & Boyd
an imprint of
Zeticula
57 St Vincent Crescent
Glasgow
G3 8NQ
Scotland.

http://www.kennedyandboyd.co.uk
admin@kennedyandboyd.co.uk

First published in 1946 in Glasgow by William MacLellan
Text Copyright © Estate of Fred Urquhart 2011
Introduction Copyright © Isobel Murray 2011

Front cover photograph © Kim Traynor 2011
Back cover photograph from Fred Urquhart's own collection
Copyright © Colin Affleck 2011

ISBN-13 978-1-84921-107-9

Introduction

Fred Urquhart

In the world of Scottish Literature, Fred Urquhart is something of an Invisible Man. With one notable exception, to which I shall return, Fred Urquhart (1912-95) was always something of a loner, an odd man out. As a boy he had no settled home, because his father, a chauffeur, took a series of jobs and moved the family to Berwickshire, Fife, Perthshire, Wigtownshire and Edinburgh. He attended a series of schools, which would have tended to break up any budding friendships for the boy. He very much disliked the last of these, Boroughmuir in Edinburgh, and consequently left school in 1927, aged fifteen. Thus he escaped the obvious path for a bright boy of proceeding to university, and forming friendships there with like-minded peers, perhaps for life. He used to deny that he had missed much, academically, as instead he worked in a bookshop for eight years, reading widely and voraciously.

He may indeed have missed some intellectual direction in this process, but he also missed the assimilation process that tended to happen, when young minds were being taught – and challenged – together. So his class origins, for example, remained clear. From early on too, he dreamt of being a writer, and wrote two unpublished novels in his teens. This is of course a solitary occupation. He tells in a memoir about his early love of the cinema, 'my love affair with the cinema', and 'my long cinematic amour.' Cinema could be said to be a national pastime in the thirties and forties.[1]

He left Scotland before the end of the war in 1944, and did not live there as a permanency again until after his partner's death in 1990. So from 1944 to 1990 he was effectively a stranger, although thinking still in Scots, as he said. But, given freedom of choice when the war was over, he gravitated to London. He had been aware of his homosexual leanings for years, and the early unpublished novels are preoccupied with homosexual feelings. It was natural for him to move to London, where there was a flourishing gay underworld centred on Soho and Fitzrovia, where bohemian artists and writers of like mind also congregated. He cites:

> Nina Hamnett, Sylvia Gough, Nina's rival for the queenship of Soho, Robert MacBryde and Robert Colquohoun and John Minton, the artists, all old friends of mine, as well as Vernon Scannell, Dylan Thomas, Julian Maclaren Ross, Rhys Davies,. . . and many other well-known Soho characters.[2]

Of course, homosexuality was not actually legalised in England until 1967, but general attitudes, especially in cities, were more accepting. In Scotland it was a crime until 1980, and attitudes change only very slowly. In an editor's Introduction, Urquhart called the Scots 'a dogmatic and complacent race', although he still aligned himself mentally with Scottish writers, many of whom had, he said, 'infinitely more gusto, passion, rumbustiousness and vigour' than English ones. From 1936 he was writing short stories for a lucrative market in little magazines, but unfortunately this market dried up after the war, and he was kept busy reading for publishers, reviewing and generally dealing with books.

His working-class Edinburgh background was important to him, and is clearly reflected in his first novel, *Time Will Knit*, 1938. The family is raised to abominate war, but when faced with the Great War, brothers react differently to the need to fight, as in his own generation. From that class and that generation, and even more from his own independent thinking, Urquhart became a declared Pacifist – not a popular position. His distaste for war is reflected in many of the stories here. He determined to register as a conscientious objector, before even realising quite how unpopular the position was. Later he was given a hard time, and remained tight-lipped about it all, but in 1941 he wrote an account of the tribunal that refused his case.

> I had said that I thought war the greatest of all evils, and that any good which might come out of it was out of all proportion to the damage that it did. . . . I'd tried to define my hatred of war in . . . my published books.[3]

He added that he should have said,' I could best help the country by continuing to be a writer.' Instead, he was to be an agricultural worker, and was sent to the Mearns, near Laurencekirk. His characteristic willingness to listen rather than hold forth is no doubt responsible for his extraordinary grasp of the local dialect, and the remarkable short stories of the Mearns he produced. In all his stories he displayed his grasp of class consciousness within the working class, town or country, and in the variations of dialect used by individuals. In the Second World War, just as in *Time Will Knit*, two brothers went to war and one stayed away, but there was no family disagreement:

> I was determined I was not going out. Fight Hitler my own way. Because Hitler is here. There are still a lot of people here and still nothing between them and Hitler, except Hitler did persecute the Jews.[4]

The notable exception to his being a loner and an odd man out took place in 1947, when he met Peter Wyndham Allen on 25th May 1947:

> We fell in love, and we lived together for forty-three years until he died, aged eighty-two, on 9th November 1990. It was a very happy homosexual marriage.'[5]

Thereafter Urquhart was the bread-winner and Wyndham Allen the housekeeper, as his account confirms, and they lived quietly in the country for the most part. Urquhart was somewhat agoraphobic, and isolation suited him: 'In England I lived on the outskirts of a forest for thirty-three years, and for weeks on end I never saw a soul.' [6] When his partner died in 1990 Urquhart returned to Scotland, to live near his brother and his wife in Musselburgh.

The Clouds Are Big with Mercy

The book was published by William MacLellan in Glasgow in 1946, and the stories were written between

1937 and 1943. Given this, it was inevitable that war is at least an intrusive background to many of the stories.

As time went on, Urquhart tended to preface a collection of stories with a novella, a slightly fuller treatment, and I would like to deal here separately with the one he gives here, although it is little more than fifty pages long.

Namiętność: or The Laundry Girl and the Pole

This story manages to be very personal and individual, and yet have a universal meaning. Urquhart was living in Cupar when he wrote it, between October 1940 and New Year's Day, 1941. He observed the antics of the local girls and the Polish soldiers based in the town. Already Urquhart has seized on what will be a major topic in his wartime stories – romance between local Scottish girls and a shifting population of troops posted nearby, English, Polish or whatever. The universality is indicated by the novella being translated during the war into Polish: it was serialised in *Dziennik Zolnierza*, the Polish soldiers' daily. It is of course a story almost as old as time, but Urquhart did much to record the war of his own time.

The main character is the laundry girl, Nettie Douglas, who is found at the start, one of a crowd of girls, each boasting about 'her own adventures' the night before, outside the laundry. Urquhart rarely spends space on description, relying mainly on inner thoughts and dialogue, so the beginning is important to reveal the author's attitude. He is careful not to glamorise the girls: this description for example underlines their idolatry of film, their lack of hygiene, and an abiding second-hand quality:

ix

They were a tough-looking lot. Their appearances were modelled on the appearances of their favourite film stars, sometimes two stars fighting for supremacy in the get-up of a girl who was like neither. A Garbo bob and a Joan Crawford mouth sat oddly on the face of a girl with a snub, almost flat, nose. And as most of them had not washed their faces or had, at the most, given them only a cursory lick and a slap with a powder-puff, most of them had an almost second-hand look in the dull autumn morning light. Shoddy caricatures of the glamorous girls on stills outside cinemas though they were, still there was an animation about them. (page 7)

After this description, which suggests comedy but a certain sympathy with the girls, we have to rely for the most part on dialogue. Gradually we learn that Blytheden is a town where there is little to do in the way of entertainment. Two cinemas, with films based on romantic fantasy, popular songs from the radio that the girls all know by heart, great evenings at the chip shop, more or less limit their activities – they are strictly forbidden alcohol and the wicked unknown of hotels.

The comedy permeates the piece, in all sorts of different ways. The girls tend all to react together to any event, and discuss it in their native, muscular prose, with quick reversals, or insights that mean more than they know: staring out a high window, Meg laments: 'They all look alike. Ye cannae make them oot at this distance', (10) and Aggie says, 'They just look the same as oor ain sodgers, except that they've got Poland in red on their shoothers'. (12) As the English soldiers marched to the station, they sang *Roll Out The Barrel,* and when the Poles march in, 'The voices rose clearly, singing *Roll Out The Barrel!'* (13) The comic difficulties raised by attempted translations are legion. There is something very funny about the would-be ravishers throwing money away to stuff the girls with chips, alcohol being unavailable. But to the reader it is clear almost from the start what the Poles are after:

'Beautiful Scottish girl, I love you. . . . I love you. All the same, all countries.' And he put his hand on Meg's knee, winking suggestively. (20)

When Nettie's sister Chrissie plays with Bert the chipman's cat, the humour – and the implication – seems to go over her head:

'Do ye no' like pussies?' Chrissie cried.
'Pussee!' he laughed. 'Veree nice.' (34)

The novella is near-perfectly written. But a sign of Urquhart's ongoing apprenticeship as a writer is perhaps the odd intervention by the narrator with his 'moral message'. Interestingly, it is not directly about sex education! It is political, although hardly spelt out. The first intervention concerns the film of *The Grapes of Wrath.* Nettie's father doesn't fancy it – 'It's a picter aboot puir folk. . . We see enough o' that aboot oor ain doors wi'oot goin' to see it on the picters' (50). Nettie is in such a panic about Jan's possible posting to Egypt that she has no time for it: 'It was just another picture. Nothing to do with her and Jan.' (53) Urquhart intervenes to say this:

Although they in their way were starving, too: as much driven and harassed as the people in the film. The Netties and Jans of this world are legion. It is because the Netties and Jans are like this that films like *The Grapes of Wrath* must be made to show why wars like this happen. (53)

A few pages later, we find Nettie 'in a state of drunken sentimentality,' dreaming of a golden future:

In hundreds of places in Britain young couples were sitting, listening to this promise of a better world. . . . None of them ever thought that for one couple for whom the world would glow with gold and glory a hundred couples would never live under any skies but skies of grey. Or if they thought about it, they imagined that *they* would be the fortunate couple. (57)

And all this takes place during an air-raid!

Repeatedly these or girls like them will be Urquhart's subjects, hard up, ignorant, uneducated, with little to look forward to, and with the excitement of the influx of foreign soldiers with money in their pockets. In his book *Love, Sex and War: Changing Values 1939-45*, John Cost reflects on the fates of some of these victims of war:

Some were adolescent girls who had drifted away from homes which offered neither guidance or warmth and security. . . . There were decent and serious, superficial and flighty, irresponsible and incorrigible girls among them. There were some who had formed serious attachments and hoped to marry. There were others who had a single lapse,often under the influence of drink. There were, too, the 'good-time girls' who thrived on the presence of well-paid servicemen from overseas, and semi-prostitutes with little moral restraint. But for the war many of these girls, whatever their type, would never have had illegitimate children.[7]

But Urquhart's narrative does not, on the surface, treat the subject so seriously. Although they all know what not to do, the girls show frightening confidence in their ability to cope, and they are matched with much more practised partners. The excitement of this unreal and novel situation fills them all, and they learn quickly to change partners in the dance of war. Nettie was madly in love with the departing Cockney soldier Harry and his warm but not over venturous love-making before she met Polish Jan (who seduces her with polished ease and a measure of alcohol), but by the end she can't find time to read Harry's letters.

The girls are all aware that they must take care how far the love-making goes. But the Poles soon ask The Question, and disarray ensues. The Question comes too late for Nettie. She has discovered *namiętność* – passion, or infatuation – with Jan, and can't think about the trades union, or the future, or anything. Only one thing can crack this – the sudden, appalling fear that she may be pregnant. Her ignorance only adds to her panic, and she vows to have done with Jan for good. The climax occurs in the dry closet at the foot of the garden when she lights the candle; and it is brilliantly underplayed. This time she is lucky, as she comes in singing, off to meet her predatory Pole once more.

After the bulk of Urquhart's first book of short stories, *I Fell for a Sailor*, was lost in the Blitz, these stories were published in 1946. The time gap was inevitable, what with paper shortages. But it means that the stories in *The Clouds Are Big with Mercy* served to remind people who had gone through it all of the national feeling at the start of the war. And of course they are now newly informative to generations that never experienced the war. All the elements are here, in a set of kaleidoscopic pictures; most importantly, the Blackout, and how it changed young peoples' lives; and air raids and shelters and sirens, and young men waiting for call up, and attractive foreign uniforms. I find them variously successful.

A couple of attempts at some sort of fable are rather stilted. 'The Big Apple' was a dance craze that swept through young people from America in 1937, and is graphically described at the end of the story. It offers a critique of current literature, from three very young, very world-weary would-be writers, and pinpoints the only kind of books that are having popular success; it points out the ubiquity and lack of identity of the cafe and the American music. It amounts to an early protest against cultural globalisation, but it lacks the animation that occurs in Urquhart whenever he is dealing with fully human individuals. Similarly, 'No Experience' deals with a quasi-universal young man whose search for work is thwarted by his lack of experience, an all-too-common situation. Even after his death, St Peter, Old Nick and a kind of Limbo offer no admittance. When he returns to life in desperation, he is readily accepted by the army, who will happily provide the experience.

The wartime stories that most appeal to me are not in the highminded manner of 'The Sands of Dunkirk' either, but pictures of working-class people coming to some sort of terms with the new conditions – 'Blackout', 'Not so Pretty Polly', 'Private War' and 'Dirty Minnie'. There is a comic realism about the suffering of young Stanley in 'Blackout', as he tries to extricate Joan from her house and into the blessed blackout; and Joan's mother's anxiety about getting the blackout right; and the family pondering it all, with apparent zeal to see the unwilling Stanley sent to the Front. 'Not So Pretty Polly' is a dirty and many would say disgraceful old woman who steals and cheats to fund her betting, and 'carries on' sexually with an equally dirty and unattractive old man: but Urquhart clearly admires her vigour and determination. Dirty Minnie, a character who will survive into Urquhart's 1949 novel, *The Ferret Was Abraham's Daughter,* has many of the same attributes, but is beloved by her sailor lodgers, who supply her, here and in the novel, with cigarettes and all manner of food, relish her bringing stout to the air-raid shelter, and giving them a 'home from home' like they never had before. One complains indignantly about the Old Man in charge, who makes more illegally than they do: '*Our* cigarettes and tobacco! Jesus, the graft that goes on down at those docks. The Old Man's only one that's makin' a pile'. His self-righteousness adds to the comedy.

'Private War' is the story of the Johnson family's first air-raid, and Urquhart creates three memorable characters. Ma Johnson is anxious to obey all the precautions and rules, and to make sure the others do too, while Pa is unwilling to get up at all, and then so interested in watching the sky that he will not take cover, although he is eager to open out the emergency liquor in the shelter. Meantime, young Ruby rips a stocking as she enters the shelter, and can think of nothing else. She wants to go back in the house in mid-raid for another pair, and when the raid is over she cannot wait to put another pair of stockings in her handbag. 'She was completely prepared now for the next air-raid!' (163)

There are also a number of stories that interestingly offer a child's eye view of their subject matter, most notably perhaps 'The Clouds Are Big with Mercy'. This is a war story, but set in the time of the Spanish Civil War. It is quietly subtle. The child Jose's simplistic view of life and the war is anti-Fascist, to the point that he seriously wants to kill a classmate who offered a Fascist salute to threatening troops. His teacher, Don Balthazar, is rapt in the poems of William Cowper, who wrote the religious lines, 'the clouds ye so much dread / Are big with mercy.' When an air raid comes, young Jose is so far from his real self that he thanks Jesus and the Virgin that they are enemy planes. But as the young Jose pursues his murderous plan, and leads Manuel away from the rest, he stumbles and hurts his knee. A child once more, he calls Manuel, who will help him to safely, proving Cowper's message,'

> God moves in a mysterious way
> His wonders to perform.

The story is full of irony, and sacrilegious prayers, which are indeed mysteriously answered.

Impossible to discuss every story, but I want to mention three more, to indicate the range inside this slim volume. The first, 'The Matinee', shows how Urquhart shares the problems and pains of his characters. Henry, the cocksure adolescent, is marvellously portrayed centrally, wearing short pants to get into the cinema for half price. The rightwing message of the film, which he complacently endorses, is amusingly recounted. But we suffer too for little brother Ian, whom he takes along to receive a prize if he wins, and who becomes desperate to pee. He repeatedly appeals to Henry to take him out, but is ignored. Urquhart described an aunt who took him to the cinema as a little boy, 'even though, almost always, at the most exciting part of the film, I had to be taken out to pee.' [8] Meanwhile, in the film, a child lisps, 'Daddy, I'm hungry.' And Henry, immune to the desperation of his little brother, is moved with pity for the child on the screen:

> Henry sniffed sympathetically when the father drew
> his sleeve across his eyes and turned away. (112)

Urquhart *knew* both Henry's love for cinema, and Ian's ill-timed need to pee: he suggests both, unforgettably.

'The Loony' and 'Man about the House' deal with darker and more unpleasant feelings. 'The Loony' concerns a middle-aged and disappointed woman who felt humiliated by having to start drawing money from the Unemployment Exchange, the Dole. So she took on the job of caring for Miss Rhona, whom she called the Loony, an unfortunate mentally deficient and underdeveloped being who needed everything done for her, but did nothing but rock in her rocking chair. The Loony never changes, but Miss Mayfield does. At first she likes the job, but gradually she becomes infuriated by the calmness of Miss Rhona, angry, resentful, hating her stolid composure. At last this hitherto respectable woman begins to harbour murderous thoughts. She ponders different methods, and decides to push her downstairs: 'Miss Mayfield had become a completely different character.' (93) The story rises to a climax. In the magazine version, published in 1940, she carries out her murder, but in the revision she loses her nerve, and faces a fate perhaps worse than committing murder:

She realised suddenly and with horror and self-pity that this would happen again and again and that she would never have the courage to take the decisive step. (95)

'Man about the House' also reflects the reactions of a central character to something weird, frightening, unknown. The charwoman who comes to her new job encounters a pale and very watchful young man who scans her every move. His presence makes her 'vaguely uncomfortable' at first, but as time passes she becomes annoyed, irritable, acutely aware. But his mother has two stories to tell, only one when he is there. In it she finds her son's presence a great comfort, and rejoices he's never had to go out to work, but she does like a man about the house, to keep her company. But when Eric briefly goes out, her tune changes. He'll soon have to register for the army:

> 'Ach, dinnie worry aboot that,' Mrs Watt said. He doesnie look strong. They'll never take him.'
> 'It's not that I was thinking about,' Mrs Laurie said. 'I was wondering what I'd do if they didn't take him.'

She tries to persuade Mrs Watt to come as often as possible, hints previous charwomen have upset Eric, and warns of his temper. When Mrs Watt finds him silently redoing her own work, she begins to feel she needs a drink: 'No wonder his mother looked as though she was being driven potty.' She promises the mother she will return, but as she leaves the very sight of him at the window makes her panic-stricken. Here Urquhart has brilliantly induced fear of the mysterious, the uncanny, in an outwardly simple situation.

Future volumes in this series will show how Urquhart developed in the short story, the novella and the novel, a great unrecognised Scottish master of prose.

Isobel Murray

Notes

1   See 'My Many Splendoured Pavilion' in Maurice Lindsay, editor, *As I Remember: Ten Scottish Writers Recall How Writing Began for Them*, 1979, pp 170, 172.

2   See 'Forty Three Years: A Benediction' in *The Ghost of Liberace,* New Writing Scotland No 11, 1993, p 140.
3   'Let Us Endure An Hour': A Conscientious Objector in England' in *The Southern Literary Messenger,* March 1941, pp 134-5
4   From an unpublished transcript of an interview with IM in *The Scotsman,* for FU's eightieth birthday.
5   See 2 above, p 135.
6   Interview at 4 above.
7   See J Costello, *Love, Sex and War: Changing Values 1939-45,* 1985, pp 276-7.
8   'My Many Splendoured Pavilion' as at 1 above, p 166.

Thanks are due to Messrs. Faber and Faber and the Editor of Horizon *for permission to reprint "Man About The House" from* Horizon Stories. *A number of the other stories have appeared in* Cambridge Front, Life and Letters To-Day, Little Reviews Anthology: 1st Series, The New Alliance, English Story, Modern Reading, Penguin Parade, The Scots Magazine, The Spectator, Story (U.S.A.), *and* Writing To-Day, *and the usual acknowledgments are made to the editors. The novella,* Namietnosc *has been translated into Polish and has appeared serially in* Dziennik Zolnierza, *The Polish Soldiers Daily.*

CONTENTS

1. NAMIĘTNOŚĆ

THE LAUNDRY GIRL AND THE POLE

I

The English soldiers were going away. The girls stand-ing outside Scott's Snowwhite Laundry could speak about nothing else. Each of them was talking about what had happened to her the night before, but none of them was listening to the others. Each was so anxious to tell of her own adventures that she hadn't time to listen to the others, except to try to go one better.

They were a tough-looking lot. Their appearances were modelled on the appearances of their favourite film stars, sometimes two stars fighting for supremacy in the get-up of a girl who was like neither. A Garbo bob and a Joan Crawford mouth sat oddly on the face of a girl with a snub, almost flat, nose. And as most of them had not washed their faces or had, at the most, given them only a cursory lick and a slap with a powder-puff, most of them had an almost second-hand look in the dull autumn morning light. Shoddy caricatures of the glamorous girls on stills outside cinemas though they were, still there was an animation about them as they talked about the soldiers who were leaving the town that forenoon.

7

"Freddie wanted to gi'e me an engagement ring," Meg Patrick said. "But I just tellt him that I wasnie tyin' masel' doon. There was time enough for that, I said, in another five years when I've had ma fling."

"Ye'll maybe ha'e yer fling once too often," Aggie Foster said, laughing.

"Well, I'm better to do that than no' to ha'e ony fling at a'—like some folk I could mention!"

Meg jerked her head with triumph when Aggie's plain face flushed. She was preparing to say more, but she stopped when two girls joined them.

"Ay, Nettie, did ye ha'e a guid time last night?" she asked the smaller girl, who had auburn hair bunched in a mass of tangled curls above a washed-out face and a mouth hastily dabbed with lipstick. She was wearing a white waterproof, tightly belted round her thin waist, and she was clinging to the arm of a girl with a fat freckled face and a slight squint.

"Ay, I had a guid time," Nettie giggled. "What do ye think I had?"

"I thought ye'd maybe got caught," Meg said. "Ye're like a washed-oot dish-cloot. Ye surely didnie get ony sleep."

"Ach to hell, mind yer ain business." Nettie giggled and teetered into the laundry on her high-heeled black suede shoes which gave over slightly at the sides and which were caked with yesterday's mud. "Come on, Bell, let's get in or Nancy Pretty'll be on the war-path!"

"Ay, come on," Meg said, following them. "Or we'll never hear the end o' it. 'Do you girls thingk we're runnig a charity insdidudion?'" She mimicked Miss Scott's thick nasal voice. "'This is a loddry, nod a kindergarden.'"

Nettie hummed softly as she sorted her ironing-board. Back to this bloody place again! After what happened last night. . . . She leaned for a few minutes on the board, thinking about it. Then her hand plugged in her iron mechanically and she fished in the basket beside her for a garment. Better be doing something or Nancy Pretty would be saying, as she had said yesterday: "Well, are you dreamig again, Miss Douglas? Are you wonderig what

you're goig to wear when you marry the Duke of Windsor?"

Sarcastic old bitch. Nettie wished that she weren't the
boss so that she could give her a good piece of her mind.
The Duke of Windsor! No, thank you, she didn't want
any Duke of Windsor when she had Harry. *Oh, Harry, oh
Harry, how you can love! Oh Harry, oh Harry, heaven's
above.* . . . She began to press a wine-coloured costume.
This was good stuff. It belonged to that woman who lived
in the big white house on the Dunesk Road. She could be
doing with it. They said that woman had tons of money—
though if she had tons of money what would she be
bothering about getting her clothes cleaned and pressed
for? Nettie knew she wouldn't if she had tons of money.
If only Harry was able to give her things like this. *Oh
Harry, oh Harry . . . . . heaven's above . . . . . .*

She had met him in Bert's chip-shop two months ago.
He had been in Blytheden for three months and hadn't
clicked with anybody until he saw her. She didn't know
how she hadn't managed to see him before that; she had
thought she had known most of the soldiers by sight. Of
course, he was awfully shy. The wireless had been playing
Until You Fall In Love, so maybe that is what had made
him speak. He had been with some other soldiers, and she
had been with Meg and Bell and Aggie. On the prowl, as
her mother said. But she had never been on the prowl
since she met Harry. Her days for prowling were past.
Until you fall in love the nights all seem to be the same. . . .
Until you fall in love there'll be no lover's lane. . . . . .

There had been a lovers' lane last night all right! Every
English soldier in Blytheden was saying good-bye to his girl-
friend. The blackout was full of couples standing in the
queerest places, clasped together. She and Harry had been
lucky. They had stood in the corner of the road-block on
the Dunesk Road. Occasionally masked motor lights
flashed on them, but the road-block had sheltered them
from the wind. Nettie could still feel the dampness of the
bricks on her back as Harry had pressed her against them.
"You'll write to me every day, Nettie, won't you?" he had
said in that Cockney voice she had laughed at before she
had learned to understand what he was saying.

9

Of course, she would write to him. Though what she was going to write about she couldn't imagine. There would be nothing doing in a small place like Blytheden after the soldiers went away.

At ten o'clock the girls heard the soldiers begin to march past the end of the street on their way to the station. They were singing *Roll Out The Barrel!* The girls looked at Miss Scott who was sitting in the small office beside the door. Meg, who was screened by some clothes-horses, stood on top of a table and looked out of the high window. She rubbed away the steam with her elbow. "Ach, I can hardly see onythin'," she said. "They a' look alike. Ye cannie make them oot at this distance."

Bell heaved herself up beside Meg, but none of the others dared to leave their boards. Nettie leaned on hers, wondering if she could make out Harry's voice among all the others. But it was hopeless.....

"And we'll have a jolly good time!" Aggie joined in the last words of the soldiers' song as it began to fade.

Nettie sighed and gave her iron a shove. "Will we hell!"

"I wish I was goin' to Egypt wi' them," Meg said, clambering down. "I tellt Freddie. I says, 'What would ye say if I landed aside ye in the middle o' the desert?' And do ye ken what he said?"

"Somethin' dirty, I'll bet!" Aggie said. "Yon Freddie was a bit o' a lad."

"I'd better no tell ye then, seein' ye're so easy shocked." Meg damped the sheet that was spread on her board, smoothing it out with her large red hands. "I tellt him to watch his step wi' thae Egyptians. Ye never ken what tricks they'll be up to wi' their veils and whatnots. The ones I've seen on the picters were a right bad lot."

"How do ye think I'd look wi' a veil?" Aggie asked.

"It would be a big improvement. Though even wi' a veil it would need to be in the blackout!"

"Well, it would be guid enough for the Poles that are comin'," Bell said. "I wonder what they'll be like?"

"Ach, what does it matter what they're like?" Nettie said.

"They say there's to be twa thoosand o' them," Aggie said.

"There can be twenty thoosand for a' I care," Nettie said. "I'm no' botherin' aboot ony Poles." She sighed and slid her iron slowly along her board. "I'm no carin' if I never see a bloody Pole. I wish they were a' awa' back to Poland."

All forenoon she worked in a daze. She could not realize that she would not be meeting Harry tonight as usual. It would be strange not to hear the shrill English accents about the streets. There would be no more walks along the Dunesk Road with his arm around her. No more standing in the doorway every night, kissing and cuddling, until Ma yelled that it was high time she came inside. She felt sick every time she thought of how far it was to Egypt. . . . God alone knew what might happen to him there. . . . though maybe the war would be over before then. . . .

On the way home at dinner-time Elsie McClure caught up on Bell and Nettie. "I'm goin' to call a meetin' aboot a Union," she said. "The morn's night."

"Och, you and yer Union!" Nettie gave her shoulders a wriggle. "I havenie time to be bothered."

"But we should ha'e a Union," Elsie said, her pinched nose glowing in her small earnest face. "It's the only thing that'll make auld Scott sit up."

"She's mair likely to make you sit up," Bell said, uncleeking her arm from Nettie's. "Well, cheerio the now!"

Elsie continued to talk about a Union as they walked towards Nettie's door, but Nettie pranced along on her high heels, not listening. "Ach to hell, Unions are for men," she said. "What are we needin' to bother aboot a Union for?"

II

When Nettie went in she found her mother's crony, Mrs. Baxter, sitting by the fire, drinking tea.

"So yer lad's awa', Nettie," she said.

"Ay." Nettie made a face at the plate her mother was putting on the table. "Ach, mince!"

"Ay, mince!" Mrs. Douglas said. "What mair do ye expect? I'm sure I do the best I can off yer wee pay."

11

"Well, ma, ye ken I dinnie like mince."

"Dinnie well ma me! If ye want to turn up yer nose, turn it up at auld Scott. She's no' sittin' doon to mince, I'll be bound!"

"I doot ye'll ha'e to get married, Nettie," said Mrs. Baxter, laughing. "Then ye can make what ye like."

"Ay, she'll be able to make a lot off a sodger's pay!" Ma sniffed.

"Ye'll ha'e to get a Pole, Nettie," said Mrs. Baxter.

"I'll Pole her!" Ma said. "There are no Poles comin' here. I dinnie trust thae foreigners. They're here to-day and gone to-morrow. A lot o' ruffians."

"Well, they're better than the French," Mrs. Baxter said.

"Ay, the French are very deceitful. All the same, it's no' right puttin' thae foreigners among decent folk." Ma poured herself another cup of tea and drank it, standing with her back to the fire, her bony elbows stuck out aggressively.

"They tell me the Poles get nine shillin's a day," Mrs. Baxter said, holding out her empty cup for more tea.

"Harry'll ha'e to join the Polish army!" Nettie laughed. "He'd think he was a millionaire on nine bob a day."

"Ach, that cannie be true," Ma said. "Nine bob a day. It's ridiculous!"

"Harry could gi'e me six," Nettie said.

"Ye could eat what ye liked then." Ma lifted her empty plate. "Though I see ye've snapped up a' yer mince whether ye liked it or no'."

"I saw some Poles this forenoon," Mrs. Baxter said. "Some o' the scoutin' party. There's some nice lookin' fellies among them. I wouldnie mind bein' your age again, Nettie!"

"I'm no' botherin' aboot them." Nettie filled a cup with tea. "I'm havin' nothin' to do wi' ony Poles."

III

But all the other girls were talking about the Poles that afternoon. Some of them had seen a company coming off a train. "They just look the same as oor ain sodgers." Aggie said. "Except that they've got Poland in red on their shoothers."

"What did ye expect them to look like?" Meg jeered. "Fifth Columnists?"

"Ach, she wouldnie ken a Fifth Columnist if she saw one," Bell said.

"She's seen Nancy Pretty, hasn't she?" Meg looked about to see that Miss Scott wasn't within hearing. "Though *she's* mair like a Cooper's Snooper, aye spyin' on folk."

Nettie didn't listen to them much. She wasn't interested in the Poles. She worked steadily, humming softly to herself, a half-smile on her face.

A burst of singing from outside made her stop ironing and look up.

"What's that?" somebody cried.

"It'll be mair Poles comin' off the train."

The girls made an involuntary movement towards the door, but when Miss Scott came out of the office they picked up their irons again, bending their backs.

The voices rose clearly, singing *Roll Out The Barrel!* The girls looked at each other. "Goodness!" Meg said. "For a meenit I thought it was oor ain sodgers comin' back again."

" Fancy them bein' able to sing English!" Aggie said.

" The English couldnie sing like that," Bell said. " They're far better singers than the English."

The girls argued about this, but Nettie did not bother to say anything. She knew that the English were far, far better singers than the Poles. All the same, it was nice to hear them. She hummed the tune.

There was a pause after the last words, then the Poles began to sing something that none of the girls knew. There was a foreign sound about it, nostalgic and forlorn. The voices rose and fell plaintively. . . . .

" What in the name o' God's that?" Meg asked.

Miss Scott was standing alone at the door, looking out. She turned when she heard Meg's question, a sarcastic smile on her thin sallow face. "If you girls lisdened to the wireless on Sunday nights instead of gallivanting," she said, "you'd know id was the Polish National Anthem."

IV.

" I think I'll wash ma hair," Nettie said after she had finished her tea. " Bell's comin' for me at eight o'clock. I'll just ha'e time to do it afore she comes."

She began to run water into the sink, but her young sister, Chrissie, yelled: " Ye'll do nothin' o' the kind."

" What for no'?"

" Help me to wash the dishes, ye lazy bitch. I'm wantin' to go oot, too."

" I will not," Nettie said.

" Ye will sut!" Chrissie ran to the bedroom door and wailed: "Ma, she says she's goin' to wash her head!"

" I'll wash her head her!" Ma cried, coming into the kitchen. " Come on, get thae dishes washed and no' ha'e the place lookin' like a pigsty."

" Ach to hell," Nettie whined.

" Come on," Ma said. " Ye ken what a time ye take when ye wash yer head. Ye can easy do that on Sunday. Ye can rise early and get it a' ower afore the rest o' us are up."

Nettie snivelled sulkily while she helped her sister to wash the dishes. Chrissie said nothing; she clattered about, her high heels tapping triumphantly on the faded linoleum. Nettie was stacking the last plates in the cupboard when Bell knocked at the door and walked in.

" Are ye no' ready yet?" she said.

" I'll just be a meenit." Nettie put on her white waterproof and gave her face a few dabs with her powder-puff. " Okay!"

" Have ye got yer torch?" Ma yelled after them.

Nettie felt in her pocket. " No, but I'm no' needin' it."

" Well, if ye get knocked doon in the blackout, dinnie blame me. Dinnie say I didnie warn ye. See and come hame in time and no' be stravaigin' the streets to a' 'oors. Mind there might be a warnin'."

" A' right." Nettie slammed the door behind her and slipped her arm through Bell's. They stood for a second, letting their eyes become accustomed to the blackout. Then leaning against each other, they made for the main street, their high heels pattering along the pavement. Nettie wished it was Harry's arm she was clinging to and Harry's shoulder she was touching. There was a soft flabbiness about Bell's shoulder that made her feel that if Bell were to lurch slightly on her high heels they would both fall.

" Will we go to the picters?" she said.

" I've no money," Bell said. " I've seen the one in the Scala onyway, and I dinnie fancy the one in the Ritz."

" What'll we do then?"

" We'll just gang for a walk."

" Ach to hell," Nettie said.

But they walked on, along the main street, along the Chapelgate, back on the main street again. It was pitch dark, but there was plenty of people about. They could hear voices and laughter and the clatter of soldiers' heavy boots.

It began to rain. " I kent this would happen," Bell said. " It's felt like rain a' night."

They stood in the doorway of Veitch the grocers. Nettie remembered how often they had stood there before she had met Harry; in the blackout, waiting for something to turn up; and before the war when the street lamps let you see everybody. " Oh, come on hame," she said. " Let's go hame."

" Och, wait a wee while," Bell said. " Listen!"

Several soldiers clattered past, talking in what the girls took to be Polish. Bell giggled and cried: " It's a lovely night!" The soldiers paused for a moment and laughed. But they clattered on.

" That crowd doesnie understand English, onyway," Bell said.

" Aw, come on hame," Nettie said.

" Ach, just a meenit. What's wrong wi' ye the night? Ye werenie aye in such a hurry."

Nettie didn't answer. What was the use of talking about Harry to Bell? She wouldn't understand. Bell was too flighty. She never bothered about a 'steady' fellow. It was funny how she managed to get them with that fat face and that shape. Harry had once called her ' the cow with the freckled corn.' *Oh Harry, Oh Harry, how you can love. . . . .*

She began to hum the tune, and Bell joined in, shaking her shoulders and pattering her feet in time. " Oh Johnnie, oh Johnnie, how you can love!" she sang the proper words. "Oh Johnnie, oh Johnnie!"

Some soldiers at the opposite side of the narrow street laughed and halted. Bell sang more loudly and began to tap-dance, giggling enticingly between the words.

"Aw, come on hame," Nettie said.

But Bell went on singing and tapping her feet. The soldiers talked to each other, laughing. One of them stepped off the pavement, but another said something and he stopped. "Good evening!" one of them called.

"Good evening!" Bell cried. "It's a lovely night!"

The soldiers laughed. "A lovelee night," they said it to each other. "A lovelee night!" They began to walk away, laughing and repeating the phrase.

"Aw, come on hame," Nettie said.

"Ach, what's a' yer hurry?"

"Well, what's the sense o' standin' here in the rain? I'm cauld."

"A' right, let's gang along to Bert's."

"Okay," Nettie said.

It was pouring now. They slithered through the spotted blackness, their bare heads bent against the rain, the soles of their cheap shoes squelching in the wet. They brushed past people hurrying like themselves. Torches flashing occasionally showed rain-stripes falling in front of wet coats and legs. There wasn't so much laughter and noise as there had been, except giggling from those in doorways.

Meg and Aggie were sitting in the back parlour of Bert's fish and chip shop. There was nobody else in the place. Meg looked up with interest when she heard the door opening, but when she saw who it was she bent again over an old copy of *John Bull*, her eyes screwed up, a cigarette in the corner of her mouth.

"It's you, is it?" she said.

"Ay, it's us," Nettie said. "Who did you think it would be? Clark Gable?"

"I wish it was!"

"No' got a Pole yet?" Bell laughed as she slumped down beside Aggie and put her fat elbows on the blue and white checked oil-cloth of the table.

"A Pole!" Meg screwed up her face even more with disgust. "There are plenty in the streets, but it's that dark that ye cannie do onythin' aboot it. There's been nobody in here but yon wee bandy-leggit man that works in the torpedo factory."

"What are ye goin' to ha'e, Nettie?" asked Bell.

"Och, I think I'll just ha'e an ice."

"It's no' guid for yer stummick on a cauld night like this," Aggie said. "Ye need somethin' warmer."

"We ken that," Meg said, dabbing her cigarette-butt fiercely in the ash-tray which had *Take A Peg of John Begg* printed on it. "But where are we goin' to get it? I'm fed up. I'm goin' hame after I feenish ma lemonade."

"It's that bloody wet the night," Aggie said. "I wish it had been fair."

"What difference would it ha'e made to you?" Meg began to powder her face. "Come on, feenish thae chips and let's get goin'."

Nettie took a spoonful of ice-cream, then she picked up the copy of *John Bull* that Meg had laid on the table. "Ach to hell," she said. "I've read this afore. It's been here for weeks. Hey, Bert! Do ye never think o' gettin' ony new maggyzines in this dump?"

"What are ye wantin' a maggyzine for?" Meg said. "Are ye no' comin' wi' me and Aggie?"

"Ay, when I've feenished this." Nettie put a spoonful of ice-cream in her mouth, letting it lie on her tongue, relishing the flavour. "I wonder what Harry's doin'?" she said, putting her head in her hands and staring at herself in the large mirror.

"They'll be in London by this time," Bell said.

"Let's hope they dinnie get bombed," Meg said. "It would just be like Freddie to get bombed afore he went to Egypt."

Bert had switched on the wireless behind the counter. He was leaning on one fat elbow beside it, listening to the B.B.C.'s nine o'clock news.

"Aw, turn that off, Bert!" cried Nettie. "Gi'es somethin' to cheer us up, no' thae blethers. I'm fair seeck o' hearin' the news. I get it first thing in the mornin' when the auld man's havin' his breakfast. He cannie take his meat for listenin' to the seven o'clock news. Then when I come hame I hear the one o'clock news. Either that or Mrs. Baxter. I dinnie ken which is worst. Then I get it again when I come hame at six o'clock. I'm fair fed up hearin' it. They cannie tell ye onythin', onyway."

"Ay, what aboot some jazz?" Meg said.

"That's better," Bell said when Bert got a foreign station. And she snapped her fingers and shook her shoulders. "Who's little whatsit are you? Who's little boogy-boo?"

"Little gal, I'm lookin' for a pal," Aggie joined in, her long face seeming to grow longer as she widened her large mouth.

She stopped singing in the middle of the last word, her mouth staying wide open. Three Polish soldiers were coming in. Bell nudged her and sang louder, looking at the Poles as they prepared to sit down at the next table:

"Who's little whatsit are you?"

And she giggled when they saluted the girls before pulling out chairs.

Nettie, still staring at her reflection, glanced at the soldiers unslinging their gas-masks and taking off their heavy coats, shaking off the rain. They weren't bad looking fellows. That dark one now. She took another spoonful of ice-cream, then she smoothed the mound of ice with the back of her spoon. She sucked in the cream on her lips, feeling its coldness sharply on her teeth.

"It's a lovely night!" Bell laughed to the soldiers.

They grinned. The tallest, a florid-faced young man with horn-rimmed glasses and close-cropped upstanding fair hair, said: "Good evening. Beautiful Scottish weather."

Meg jerked her face upwards and sent a cloud of smoke towards the ceiling. "It's lovely tell your ma!"

"Ma?" The Pole looked puzzled. "Tell ... your ... ma? Please?"

Bell and Aggie giggled. "Ye cannie explain that to him," Bell said.

"It's somethin' ma mother often says," Meg said. She looked helplessly at Nettie, but Nettie was watching the dark soldier in the mirror. He was smiling at her, not bothering about what his companion was saying to him in Polish.

The fair-haired one leaned forward and said: "Parlez-vous français?"

"Parly voo fransy!" Bell and Aggie nudged each other.

"Wee wee zambuck!" said Meg.

"Zambuck?" He shook his head. "Please?"

"Aw, skip it!" Meg said. "That's another one o' ma mother's," she said to the other girls. "I wish she was here the now, she might be able to deal wi' him."

"Oh, we'll deal wi' them all right," Bell said, and she winked at the soldiers.

The fair-haired Pole still looked puzzled, but he motioned with his hands, signifying that he would draw the tables together. They did this, then he sat down between Meg and Aggie. The smallest, who had a heavy fleshy face and thick lips, sat down beside Bell. His skin was oily, his nose broad at the tip. The dark one sat next to Nettie. They smiled at each other. He had a large mole on his right temple, and now that he was closer to her she saw that he needed a shave.

The fair-haired soldier pointed to himself: "Stanislaus." Then he pointed to the others: "Jan. Paul."

The dark-haired one was Jan.

Meg giggled and pointed to herself: "Margaret."

"Margaret?" Stanislaus said it over once or twice, then he smiled suddenly: "Ah, Marguerite!" And he looked enquiringly at Bell.

"Isabel," she said.

"Ysabelle," he said.

Bell giggled and looked coy. Stanislaus looked at Aggie. She blushed and looked down at the table. "O—Olive," she whispered.

Meg raised her eybrows at Nettie, but Nettie was making patterns with her spoon on her ice-cream. Through her eyelashes she was watching Jan's fingers drumming on the table beside her. His nails were dirty and the skin around them was coarse and ingrained.

"Olive?" Stanislaus said. "Ah, Olga!"

"Olga!" said Aggie, and she giggled and gave him a nudge.

"Please?"

19

Nettie looked up, but she did not answer Stanislaus' question. She looked at Jan and said: " Nettie."

" Nettee," he said. " Nettee!"

They smiled again at each. other. What nice teeth he's got, she thought. Different from Harry's. Harry had three false teeth at the front of his mouth and they didn't fit very well. She sighed, thinking of how often she and Harry had sat there. *Oh Harry, oh Harry. . . .*

" Chips!" Stanislaus cried. " One ... two ..." He began to count slowly. " Chips! Seven!" And he held up seven fingers to Bert.

" I couldn't eat any more," Nettie said. " No thanks."

" Please?" Stanislaus said.

" She doesn't want any," Meg said loudly, and she pointed to Nettie and shook her head. "She doesn't want any," she said again, even more loudly.

" Nie?" He looked disappointed.

" Ach, go on!" Bell said. " Ye can easy eat some chips. It's a while since ye had yer tea."

" All right." Nettie nodded, then she turned to Jan and smiled.

While they were eating the chips Stanislaus and Paul repeated all the English phrases they knew, and the girls giggled at the way they pronounced the words and at the way the phrases were jumbled together. Every now and then Stanislaus said: "Good evening, Marguerite. Beautiful Scottish girl, I love you." He was very proud of his last sentence. " Good?" he said after it. " Good?"

" Very good," Meg said, taking one of his cigarettes. " Now, what about teachin' us that in Polish?"

" In Polish?" Stanislaus grinned. " I love you. All the same, all countries." And he put his hand on Meg's knee, winking suggestively.

" Here, here, not so quick;" Meg cried. " You're a fast worker. Don't be so passionate!"

" Passion ... ate?" he said. " Passion. . . . Ah, namiet-nosc!"

" Nammy what?" said Meg. " Gee, I'd never be able to say that. It'll be easier for you to learn English than for us to learn Polish."

"I should say so!" Bell said. "It's a wonder to me that they can understand it themsels. I see that some o' the shops ha'e bills up already wi' Polish written on them. It looks terrible. Like a jig-saw puzzle."

"I think that's what he thinks he's doin'." Meg pulled Stanislaus' hand onto the table. "Now, keep it there!" she said, putting her own hands on top of it.

Jan did not join his companions in showing off their English. He ate his chips slowly, smiling at Nettie between bites. The back-parlour was filling up. Some of the other laundry-girls and girls whom Nettie knew in shops and other places came in with Polish soldiers. The wireless was turned on more loudly, but even then it could scarcely be heard above the babble of voices and laughter. There was a lot of laughter. And most of the girls spoke louder than they would have spoken normally in an effort to make the Poles understand what they were saying. Between remarks to the girls, the Polish soldiers spoke rapidly to each other, laughing gaily. Some of them began to sing a Polish song, drowning out the girl who was crooning on the wireless.

Nettie leaned back and shut her eyes, listening to the strange foreign words. There was something haunting and sad about the lilt, something that made her want to cry. She wanted to lean her head on a man's shoulder. If only Harry had been there. . . . She heard Jan humming the tune. "You like it?" he said when she opened her eyes.

"It's very nice."

"Nice?" he said. "Yes, nice! It is about Polish soldier who leaves sweetheart. To the war. Veree sad. He says he come back. *Kocham ciebie*. English, I love you."

"Ko ham sib yeah," Nettie tried to say it.

"Good." He laughed. "Veree good!"

Stanislaus swaggered to the counter and bought a bundle of bars of chocolate. He put some before each of the girls. "Good," he said. "Veree good?"

"Very good," Meg said, unwrapping a bar. She held it out to him. "Are you hungry?"

"Yes." Stanislaus winked.

Nettie unwrapped her chocolate slowly and shared it with Jan. She was glad that he was a lot quieter than Stanislaus and Paul. He spoke only occasionally, looking around sometimes and smiling when there were shrieks of laughter from the people at the other tables. Mostly he looked at Nettie, his dark eyes admiring. His thigh was pressing against hers. She began to feel a little sick, and she blamed the chocolate. Her face felt flushed, and she could feel her heart thumping. Just the way she had felt the first time she saw Harry.... But differently; yes, that had been different.....

She felt that she had to say something. So she turned to Bell and said: " Gosh, it's hot in here."

" Ay, it's gettin' a bit warm." Bell giggled. " In mair ways than one. It's time we were gettin' on oor way. It's ower crowded in here for ma taste."

The girls picked up their bags and made to rise. The three soldiers sprang up, clicking their heels and half-bowing as they pulled back the girls' chairs. " Help, I feel like royalty!" Bell giggled.

Jan put out his hand to help Nettie through the narrow space between the table and the wall. " Nettee," he said softly. " Lovelee Nettee. We go promenade? Yes?"

" Listen to that!" Bell cried. " It takes thae Poles! Tell him ye've got a lad already."

" Aw, shuttup," Nettie said. " Yer tongue's ower near yer mouth." She smiled at Jan. " Okay."

" Okay?"

" Yes," she nodded.

The girls giggled and nudged each other, drawing their coats tightly and proudly around them as they waited for the soldiers to put on their great-coats and their gas-masks. Aggie shouted cheerfully to some other girls at another table, and they shouted back: " See and be good!"

" I always am," she said, giving her head a toss.

" Ay, ye never get a chance to be onythin' else!" Meg laughed and made for the door. " Come on!"

Stanislaus and Paul and Jan saluted everybody before going out, and the other soldiers rose and saluted them. " Good-night," everybody cried. " Good-night," the girls answered. " Good-night, Bert!"

" Good-night," he called, leaning on the counter, his fat face smiling. " I'll be seein' you!"

It had stopped raining and the moon was out, though wispy black clouds were skating in front of it. The streets were like polished liquorice. Nettie stood for a second, getting her eyes accustomed to the blackout. Jan put his hand on her elbow and leaned protectingly over her. "Veree lovelee," he said softly.

Nettie giggled and picked her way carefully along the pavement. She heard her heels tapping beside the thuds of his boots. They weren't as heavy boots as Harry had worn. Harry hadn't been as big as Jan, but he had made an awful noise when he clumped along beside her. She looked up at Jan. His white teeth were glistening in the moonlight. "Nettee," he said, pressing her arm against his side.

There were yells and laughter from the others who were on the other side of the street. "Come on, you twa!" Meg shouted. "Get a bend on!"

Half an hour later Nettie closed the front door softly behind her. For a few seconds she kept her hand on the knob, smiling. "Dobranoc," she whispered. "Dobranoc." It was far nice than the English good-night. Though, she sighed, she wished it had been Harry she had been with. A kiss and a cuddle were better than a polite handshake and the clicking of heels. She twisted her mouth ruefully and tiptoed along the passage past the kitchen door where she could hear her father snoring in the large double-bed.

. V.

"We had a great meetin' last night," Elsie McClure said to Nettie the next morning.

"Had ye?" Nettie yawned and listlessly spread a shirt on her ironing-board. She felt tired, and she had just remembered that she hadn't written to Harry as she had promised. She must write to-night. Though she didn't know how she was going to find time, for she had said she would go to the pictures with Jan.

"Ye should ha'e been there," Elsie said.

"Ach, what guid would I ha'e done?"

"Well, it would aye ha'e been another yin," Elsie said.

Nettie yawned again. "Ach, I'm no' botherin' aboot yer auld Union."

"Ye would like yer pay up, wouldn't ye?"

"Ach, I suppose so." Nettie damped the shirt and began to iron it. "But what a hope we've got! Auld Scott'll never gi'e us a rise."

"We'll see aboot that." Elsie sniffed and gave the large clothes-basket she was carrying a dunch upwards with her knee. "We'll see," she said, and she went briskly into the wash-house, her wellington boots sucking determinedly at the stone floor.

Nettie yawned and gave her head a shake, trying to get the sleep out of her eyes. "Dobranoc," she said to herself. Well, that was one Polish word she knew! Elsie would have been better to have been out with a soldier than to have been at her old meeting. Taking up her time with a lot of nonsense!

She wondered what she would say to Harry when she wrote. There was nothing to write about. Nothing had happened since he left. She saw how silly she had been to say that she would write every day. There wasn't enough happening in a small town like Blytheden to write about.

"Have ye got thae sheets for Fergusson?" Meg shouted across to another girl.

"No, I havenie got them."

"Ye're lucky!" Bell tittered. "That's the man that aye pishes the bed, isn't it? There should be a law aboot makin' him wash his ain sheets. He likes to get them hand-finished, too! Set him up!"

"Here they are!" Aggie cried. "I've got them. Do ye want them, Meg?"

"No fear! Ye can keep them noo that ye've got them."

"Ach to hell!" Aggie made a face and began to sing in a high whining voice: "I'm nobody's baby. I wonder why?"

"Have ye looked in the mirror?" Meg cried, poking her head through the clothes hanging on a clothes-horse.

But Aggie did not take any heed. She went on singing: "Each night and day I pray the Lord up above to please send me down someone to lo-ove...."

24

"Oh, Olga!" Bell cried in what she thought was an imitation of a Pole speaking English. "Good old Olga from the Volga! Ha'e ye seen ony boatmen yet? They're lookin' for puir fish like you!"

"Ye can laugh," Aggie said, tossing her head. "I dinnie care. I would ha'e been christened Olive if I'd had ony say in it."

"But ye were dumb!"

"She's still dumb," Meg said. "No wonder she didnie get a felly o' her ain last night. If ye'd had ony gumption, Aggie Foster, ye'd ha'e got yin o' the fellies at the other tables instead o' hangin' on to us."

"I like that!" Aggie cried. "They clicked wi' me as well as wi' you, didn't they? I cannie help that there was only three o' them. Ye've got a bloody guid neck to think that they liked you ony better than they liked me."

"Aw, what's the guid o' quarrellin' aboot them?" Bell said. "They're just Poles."

"Just Poles!" Meg laughed. "I like that Stanny What-daeyecahim. He's a right go-ahead felly."

"Maybe he's ower go-ahead," Aggie sniffed, "Ye'd better watch yersel'."

"Oh, I'll dae that. I'm able to take care o' ony o' them. The only yin I'd be a bit careful wi' is that dark yin. He's a right sleekit lookin' soul. I wouldnie trust him as far as I could throw him."

Nettie had not been paying much attention to the catter-battering of the other girls, but when she heard that she banged down her iron and looked across fiercely at Meg. "That's enough frae you, Meg Patrick," she cried. "There's nothin' wrong wi' him. He's a far nicer felly than that Stanny."

"A' right, a' right," Meg said. "Keep yer hair on! He's no' ma cup o' tea, that's all. Ye've no' been long in forget-ting Harry."

"Whae said I'd forgotten Harry? Whae spoke to the Poles first, onyway?"

"Is this all you girls have god to do?" Miss Scott poked her head out of the office.

Nettie picked up her iron and pushed it backwards and forwards furiously. Scowling at Meg, she wished that she was ramming the iron down Meg's throat. She had a right good cheek to say that about Harry. She couldn't help it, could she, if Jan clamped himself on to her? It wasn't so easy to tell him that she had a lad already with him not speaking much English and being so quiet. Nettie pulled a kirby-grip from amongst the curls at the back of her head and pushed it into one that was dangling in front of her eyes. He was not sleekit-looking. The fellow couldn't help being quiet. He hadn't a chance to get a word in edgeways when that Stanny was there.

"Well, what about it?"

Elsie McClure's voice behind her made Nettie start. She clicked her tongue irritably against her teeth as she folded a shirt and hung it on the clothes-horse. "Ach to hell," she said. "Is this you again?"

"Ay, it's me again." Elsie looked to see that Miss Scott wasn't watching from the office. "Will I put yer name doon?"

"What guid would it dae?"

"It'll dae a lot o' guid," Elsie said. "The mair names we get the better chance we'll ha'e o' gettin' oor pays up."

"Ay, the better chance we'll ha'e o' gettin' oor books!" Nettie picked another shirt out of the basket and spread it on her board. "That's what we'll get—oor walkin' tickets!"

Elsie's thin nostrils whitened as she sniffed belligerently. "Are ye feared?"

"No, I'm no' feared. But I think yer Union's a lot o' baloney."

"Ach, what are ye narkin' aboot?" cried Elsie. "It's all very well for you. Ye've got a father in steady work. It's different for a lot o' us that ha'e to keep oorsels on oor skittery wee pays."

"Oh, is it?" Nettie said, slapping the damp shirt smooth with the palms of her hands. "Ma faither's maybe in steady work, but he doesnie ha'e a big pay."

"Whae's fault is that?" Elsie said. "If he'd ony sense he'd be in a Union."

"He doesnie haud wi' Unions."

"Some folk would cut off their noses to spite their faces."

"You leave ma faither oot o' this," Nettie said.

"A' right. I suppose I'll ha'e to leave you oot o' it, too. You kind are a' alike. Ye're no' willin' to dae onythin' aboot it, but ye're there to take the pickin's wi' the rest."

"Is that so?" Nettie said.

"Ay, that's so!"

Nettie sighed wearily. "A' right. Seein' that's the way ye look at it, ye can put ma name doon."

VI.

Nettie was preparing to go to meet Jan when she remembered that she had not written to Harry. Ach to hell, she thought, I'll write to-morrow.

"Ye're surely toshin' yersel' up the night!" Chrissie jeered. "Are ye goin' somewhere special?"

"Mind yer ain business," Nettie said, peering into the small dingy mirror that hung beside the kitchen sink. She was smearing mascara on her eye-lashes, trying to see that she put it on evenly and watching that her sister didn't jolt against her on her way to and from the table with the dirty dishes. "Mind ma elbow!" she cried.

"Ye're awfu' parteecler," Chrissie said. "Ye're no' dollin' yersel' up like that just to go oot wi' Bell Waddell."

"Aw, shuttup!" Nettie said, giving her curls a last pat into place.

Chrissie giggled: "Bell wouldnie be able to see what ye looked like, onyway, wi' her keek-up-funny!" She crossed her eyes in an exaggerated imitation of Bell. "Her fellies must ha'e a job wi' her," she said, shaking some soap-powder into the sink and stirring it among the water. "They'll never ken whether she's lookin' at them or at the fellies next to them."

"Aw, shuttup," Nettie said. "It doesnie matter to you whae I'm goin' oot wi'. It's enough that I'm goin' oot."

"Well, dinnie be as late as ye were last night," Mrs. Douglas said, looking up from darning her husband's socks. "None o' ye ever seem to think ye should spend a night at hame occasionally and keep me company."

"Ach," Nettie said.

"Ay ach!" said her mother. "Ye're aye oot gallivantin'. Baith o' ye. Ye never seem to think ye should warm a seat in the hoose."

Nettie said nothing. She put on her Sunday coat: a green tweed with a red fleck in it. "What are ye puttin' that on for?" Ma said. "I'm sure yer waterproof's guid enough to go and sit in an auld dirty picter-hoose."

"Whae said I was goin' to the picters?" Nettie said.

"Well, wherever ye're goin'. Mind, ye'll no' get another new coat in a hurry. God knows if ye'll ever get a new coat again if this war lasts."

"Ach, we'll chance it," Nettie laughed. "Well, I'm away! Cheerio, ma!"

"Cheerio!" Ma said.

"Tell him I was askin' for him," Chrissie shouted after her.

Jan was waiting at the corner. Even in the blackout Nettie knew it was him before he clicked his heels and said: "Good eveneeng, Nettee."

"Hello," she said.

"'Ello!" He laughed and took her arm. "'Ello! 'Ello!"

He pressed her arm against his side, holding her hand in his and squeezing it. He said something in Polish. Nettie said, "Eh?" He laughed, evidently unable to say what he wanted to say in English. Nettie realized suddenly that there were no Stanislaus and Paul here to-night, no Meg and Bell to give her confidence. She was alone in the blackout with a strange man who spoke a different language. She wondered what she could talk about. She had never felt tongue-tied like this with Harry. Though she supposed it didn't really matter whether she knew what Jan was saying or not. It wouldn't make any difference. After all, Harry was her real lad.

As they walked along the main street Jan bent down and whispered over and over again: "Beautiful Scottish girl" and "Lovelee lovelee Nettee." Every time he said them Nettie giggled and said "Get away!" or "Ach, you're loopy!" And both of them laughed at his attempts to repeat these phrases.

There was a lot of Polish soldiers going into the picture house with girls whom Nettie knew. Jan took his place in the small queue at the pay-box. Nettie stood on the stairs leading to the balcony. She opened her handbag and looked at her face in the mirror inside. Shutting it with a satisfied smile she put it back under her arm. A girl whom she knew was standing on another step. They raised their eyebrows to each other when a young girl hurried guiltily past them, a Polish soldier following. "God, she's starting early enough, isn't she?" the other girl said.

"Ay," Nettie said. "She's just left the school. She cannie be ony mair than fourteen."

"And marchin' in here as if she had been marchin' in afore men all her life!"

Nettie shook her head, thinking that it wasn't fair that a bairn like that should get a man while girls like Aggie Foster couldn't get one. "If I was her mother I'd dae somethin' aboot it," she said.

"So would I," the other girl said, and she turned with a smile to a Polish soldier who shepherded her upstairs in front of him.

Nettie saw that Jan had got the tickets, and she prepared to go upstairs. But he grinned and nodded towards the Gentlemen's Lavatory. "I go in here."

She walked on upstairs, thinking that Harry would never have done that. Harry would have burst himself rather than do a thing like that. It was so broad, so public. She hoped that nobody had noticed.

"Hello, Nettie," the attendant said.

"Hello." Nettie leaned against the wall.

"Is yer bloke away?"

"No, he's downstairs, gettin' the tickets."

"Oh, did he no' go away wi' the rest o' the regiment?"

"Eh?" Nettie said. "Oh ay, ye mean Harry! Harry's away."

The attendant grinned. "The Poles are awful nice, aren't they?" she said. "They're awful mannerly. Ye know, I like them a lot better than oor ain sodgers. There's no use sayin' one thing and thinkin' another."

Jan came upstairs, smiling. He clicked his heels and bowed slightly when he handed the tickets to the attendant. "Good seats, yes?" he said.

The girl nodded, flushing when he slipped a tip into her hand. "Oh thanks, thanks a lot!"

Nettie followed the beam of the attendant's torch into the darkness of the back row. As they sat down Jan put his arm around her waist. . . . .

VII.

After the pictures they went to Bert's. The back parlour was crowded. They squeezed their way between the tables to the corner where Meg and Bell were sitting with Stanislaus and Paul. "Was it a guid picter?" Meg asked.

"Ach, no' bad," Nettie said. She smiled at Jan who was holding a chair ready for her. "Thanks."

"What like was Myrna Loy?" Bell said.

"Ach, no' bad," Nettie said. "Just the same as usual I suppose."

"What was she wearin'?"

"I dinnie ken," Nettie said. "I didnie notice much."

"Ye dinnie ken!" Meg nudged Bell, and they giggled.

"There's nothin' to laugh aboot," Nettie said, hunching her shoulders. "It was just an ordinary picter."

"Where have you been?" she asked Meg.

Meg rolled her eyes. "Where have I no' been!" she gurgled. "Me and Stanny went for a walk. Didn't we, Stanny? Didn't we promenade?"

"Promenade!" He leered at her, winking to the others. "Lovelee promenade! Lovelee Marguerite!"

He groped under the table, and Meg pushed away his hand, giggling. They sparred with each other. Bell began to shake her fat shoulders and hum the words of the song the wireless was playing. "You'll never hear the bluebird singing in the sky above. You'll never know the thrill until you fall. . . . ."

She stopped suddenly and gaped at the door. "Help, look at this!"

Aggie Foster was coming in, grinning with mingled embarrassment and pride. A tall Polish sergeant followed her, one hand possessively on the small of her back. He had a sullen light brown face with deep lines grooved from his nostrils to his chin. He was one of the tallest Poles Nettie had seen; taller even than Jan. Aggie came towards them, giggling nervously; she kept looking from one to the other, unsure of what they would say.

" Hello, Olga!" Bell said.

" Hello, Aggie," Nettie smiled and edged nearer to Jan. " There's plenty of room here."

The sergeant clicked his heels and saluted. Stanislaus said something in Polish to him. All the other soldiers laughed, but the sergeant just twisted his lips a little and shrugged. He said something: a few curt-sounding words. Stanislaus started to laugh, but he stopped when he saw that nobody was backing him up. Nettie looked enquiringly at Jan, but he just smiled at her.. She felt annoyed. What did they need to speak their old Polish for? Could they not speak English like other folk?

" Hya, toots!"

Somebody slapped Nettie's shoulder. It was Chrissie. A Polish soldier standing behind her sister winked at Nettie. She disliked him immediately.

" Any room for us here?" Chrissie cried. " Get ower the bed a bit, Bell, and let me and the boy-friend in!"

There was much giggling and pushing as they shifted to make room for Chrissie and the soldier. " Sit here wis me," Stanny said, putting his arm around Chrissie's waist and drawing her onto a chair. " You are safe here, yes!"

" You bet I'm safe," Chrissie cried. " But I wouldnie trust ye if the lights werenie on!"

Nettie joined in the laughter, but she did not feel like laughing; she felt irritated and annoyed. Irritated because there was such a crowd when she would have preferred to be alone with Jan. And annoyed because of Chrissie. She didn't like the look of that Pole Chrissie was with at all. She remembered the young kid she had seen going into the picture house. Of course, Chrissie was seventeen. She was able enough to look after herself. But the Pole was a lot older than that. He looked the kind who would have a wife and a large family in Poland. You never knew.

" Chips, Nettee," Jan said, pushing a plateful in front of her. " Good?"

" Good," she said.

She wouldn't have minded if Chrissie had taken up with the likes of that Stanny now. Although he was a bit of a spark, Chrissie would have been able to manage him all right. But this man was different. She looked at his low furrowed brow and small dark eyes. He saw her watching him, and he grinned, showing tobacco-stained teeth with rotten stumps at the side. If it weren't for his teeth he wouldn't be too bad-looking. But he was far too old for Chrissie. Far too old for any of them. Even Aggie's sergeant was younger than him, and he must be getting on for thirty.

" Bert's doin' a roarin' trade, isn't he?" Meg said.

Nettie nodded. Bert's was the only place open at night in Blytheden unless the bar-parlours of the local hotels which were either too expensive for most of the soldiers—even although their pays were reputed to be so large—or places to which most of the girls did not want to go. Meg said to Nettie that Stanislaus had wanted to take her and Bell to the Royal Hotel. He had flashed a few pound-notes at them and said: " Plentee of monee! " " But we werenie havin' ony," Meg said. " We didnie want folk to think that we were in the same boat as lassies like Bunty Robertson and Dolly Lindsay. Ma mother would kill me if she heard that I'd been in the Royal bar."

The place was so packed that Bert could not get near his customers, and plates of fish and chips were being passed from the counter to all parts of the room by a chain of hands. The wireless was turned on at its fullest volume, but there was so much laughter and talk that it could scarcely be heard. Most of the laughter came from the girls; they giggled at the pitch of their voices. The soldiers talked to each other in Polish, eyeing the girls and smiling.

Nettie felt that they were all marking time. That's what they were all doing—except Jan. He was different. But all the others were just out to get what they could get. Sitting there and watching the girls eating what they were paying for. . . .

" Listen! " Bell cried, cocking her head towards the wireless. " Am I hearin' right? Is that song called *Are You Happy at your Work?*"

" Ay," Meg said. " Have ye no' heard it afore?"

" It's a song that was written specially for munition-workers," Aggie said.

"To make them Go To It!" Meg said. "And Stay At It!"

"Help!" Bell shook her head. "I can hardly believe it."

"Are you happy at your work?" Aggie sang. "Sure we are! Are you gonna carry on? Sure we are!"

"Huh, there's nothin' else for it," Meg said. "We've got to carry on whether we like it or no'."

"Ay, auld Scott sees to that."

"She's a right auld skinflint," Meg said. "It's high time we had oor pays up. I just hope that Elsie McClure manages to get a Union started."

"Wheesht!" Nettie whispered. "There's Maisie Forbes ower there. She'll hear ye. Ye ken fine what a clipe she is, aye goin' to Nancy Pretty wi' tales."

"Are you happy at your work?" Aggie whined, then she winked at the sergeant and blushed. "Sure we are!"

"Work?" Stanislaus said. "Where you work?"

"In a laundry," Meg said.

"Laundree?"

"Ay, a wash-house." Meg took a plate and pushed it backwards and forwards, pretending she was ironing.

"Rub a dub dub!" Bell cried, imitating a woman at a scrubbing-board. "Three men in a tub!"

"Tub?" Stanislaus said.

"Clean clothes," Meg said.

Stanislaus' brows were knitted above the bridge of his nose. Suddenly the wrinkles sprang back like a star exploding. "Ah, prania! " he cried. "Prania!"

"Prania." The girls giggled as they tried to pronounce the word.

"We go now, Nettee? Promenade?" Jan's arm was clamped around her waist, his finger-tips touching her breast.

"Yes," she whispered, thinking of the sensations those fingers had given her in the cinema, wondering what promises they held in store for her when they got outside alone..... She stood up, buttoning her coat, eager to get away. She had not looked at Chrissie and her soldier for a while; she had tried to keep looking in other directions, telling herself that it was none of her business and that Chrissie was perfectly able to look after herself. It had not been difficult with Jan there beside her to forget everything but him. But now she could not help looking when she heard them giggling and when she heard Chrissie exclaim with disgust:

"Ach, ye've been eating fish! I can smell yer breath!"

Nettie saw that they were playing with Bert's cat. Chrissie was holding it in her arms, holding it towards the soldier. He drew back slightly, giving the cat a little poke with his forefinger.

"Do ye no' like pussies?" Chrissie cried.

"Pussee!" He laughed. "Veree nice."

"Are ye goin'?" Meg looked surprised when she saw Nettie and Jan standing. "What's a' yer hurry? Wait for us!"

"Ay, we'd better all get on the road," Bell said, rising. "I dinnie want to lose ma beauty sleep!"

"Ay, ye need a' ye can get!" Meg laughed.

VIII.

"So ye've got a Pole, Nettie!" Mrs. Baxter cried jovially when Nettie went home for dinner the next day.

"Ay," Nettie said, sitting down at the table.

"Chrissie's got yin, too," Ma said. "There was a fair regiment o' them at the door last night. Their faither was oot wi' the Home Guard and I was sittin' here masel' when I heard a lot o' guffawin' and talk. So I went oot, and here was an army lorry wi' a Pole marchin' up and doon beside it, and Nettie and Chrissie and them wi' their lads leanin' against the door. I wasnie long in shiftin' them, I can tell ye!"

Ma laughed. "I thought for a meenit that it was the Invasion!"

"I wonder if it'll come?" Mrs. Baxter said.

"We'll just ha'e to be like Asquith and wait and see!"

"There'll be an invasion o' another kind in a year or twa!" Mrs. Baxter tittered. "My word, there'll be a gey mixed breed in this part o' the country wi' a' thae foreigners. Ye'll ha'e to watch ye dinnie get ony Polish grandbairns!"

"There's no danger o' that," Ma said, and she rattled the oven-door behind her when she took out Nettie's dinner.

"Ye never know!" Mrs. Baxter laughed.

"I can trust ma lassies," Ma said. "And that's mair than a lot o' fowk can dae."

Mrs. Baxter coughed and stretched out her hand for the tea-pot. "I'll ha'e some mair tea if ye dinnie mind, Mrs. Douglas." She helped herself to milk and sugar. "I must bring ye along some sugar. I've made Andy stop takin' it in his tea."

"That'll be a help," Ma said. "I havenie got ony put by at a'."

"I wonder if things'll get ony scarcer?" Mrs. Baxter said, sighing.

"God knows! They couldnie be ony scarcer than they are the noo."

"Did ye read what auld Woolton said aboot fowk that hoarded? He said he would take a delight in dealin' wi' them."

"Ay, and it's only last week that he said on the wireless that he hoped we a' had somethin' in oor store-cupboards." Ma sniffed. "That's a' very well if ye've got a store-cupboard. Lots o' folk have got neither a cupboard nor the money to buy stuff to put into it."

"I wish it was a' ower," Mrs. Baxter said.

She sipped her tea. "Are ye goin' to the Poles' concert on Sunday? I hear that they're gi'in' it in the Scala picter-hoose. It should be guid."

"I heard their band playin' in the park the day," Ma said. "It was right bonnie."

"Ay, I heard them, too. They were playin' a lot o' Scotch tunes. My, it was lovely!" Mrs. Baxter sighed sentimentally "Ye ken, the Poles are just like the Scotch. Look at the way they sing the Scotch sangs, too!"

"They sing them a sight better than a lot o' Scotch folk I could mention," Ma said.

"Ay, I daresay," said Mrs. Baxter.

"I was speakin' to auld Jessie Petrie that bides in yon wee cottage oot the Dunesk Road this forenoon," Ma said. "She was tellin' me hoo much she liked the Poles singin'. She says a crood o' them were marchin' past when she was in her garden and she stood ahint a tree to watch them. She says she didnie like to stand and look too openly in case the officers didnie like her lookin' at the men."

"Fancy her!" Mrs. Baxter laughed. "She wasnie thinkin' the Poles would think she was after them, was she?"

"God knows," Ma said. "She's eighty if she's a day. And what a stinkin' breath she's got. Her inside must be rotten. The Poles would be made up wi' her! She's fleein' doon for her pension like a twa-year auld, beckin' and smilin' to hersel', noo that the Poles are wavin' to her."

"Wavin' to her?" Mrs. Baxter said. "They didnie wave to her, did they?"

"Of course, they waved to her. They'd wave to onythin' that had a skirt on. They're a gey lot, thae Poles."

"I'll ha'e to watch masel'," Mrs. Baxter said, tittering.

"Oh, I dinnie think they'll bother wi' the likes o' you and me, Mrs. Baxter," said Ma. "Unless it's in the black-oot! Though if auld Jessie can get a man there's aye a chance for us!"

IX.

All the girls laughed when Nettie told them about old Jessie Petrie. "Christ!" Meg said. "Imagine yon auld wife jookin' in and oot ahint trees! I'll ha'e to get Stanny to her."

"No, I think Aggie's sergeant would be the yin," Bell said. "He'd soon put the peter on her!"

"Are ye seein' him the night, Aggie?"

"You bet," Aggie simpered.

"Ye'll ha'e to watch yersel'," Meg said, winking at the others. "Ye ken what sergeants are!"

"Oh, I'll watch masel' all right," Aggie said primly.

"Where's he billeted?" Meg asked. "He's no' wi' Stanny and his crowd."

"Ye'll never guess!" Aggie giggled.

"Where?"

Aggie looked around to see that Miss Scott was nowhere in sight or hearing. "At Nancy Pretty's!"

"Ach away!"

"I'm tellin' you," Aggie said.

"God, I'm sorry for him then," Nettie said, lifting her iron. "Ye ken what auld Mrs. Scott is! She's daft wi' cleanliness,"

" Ay, it runs in the family," Meg said. " Like wooden legs! "

" I aye heard she washed her pavement," Nettie said, smoothing the pleats of a skirt carefully with the iron. " But I never believed it until the other day when I was passin' her hoose. There was a lemonade lorry at the door, and a young felly had been handin' in some bottles. Do ye ken, he was hardly on the lorry afore auld Mrs. Scott was oot wi' a cloot wipin' his feet marks off the pavement! "

" Och, she's daft," Meg said.

" She's daft a' right," Bell said. " Like her dochter! "

" I dinnie ken aboot the daftness," Nettie said. " They're no' daft enough to gi'e away ony o' their lousy money. Mrs. Penman that bides next to her tellt ma mother that she was aye cleaning' her windies."

" Ay, and do you know," Aggie said seriously, leaning forward, her long face looking even longer in its solemnity. " She makes Nancy Pretty come in the back-door and take off her shoes and put them on a newspaper."

" I wonder if she'll make yer sergeant dae that?" Meg laughed.

Aggie sniffed: " She'd better no' try it! "

" Ye'll ha'e to keep yer eye on him and Nancy Pretty! " Meg said. " She'll maybe try to pinch him frae ye! "

" She'd better no' try it either," Aggie said, and she scowled dourly at the linen sheets she was ' finishing ', pressing them savagely.

" Do ye ken what Mrs. Scott said to me the other day when I took her yon parcel?" Bell said, and she giggled. " Hell, I near fainted! "

" Well, what was it?" Meg asked. " We're no' mind-readers. No' that ye've got ony mind to read! "

" That'll dae ye, Meg Patrick," Bell said. " If I dinnie get less o' yer lip I'll no' tell ye what auld Scott said."

" A' right," Meg said. " Ye ken that I didnie mean it."

Bell sniffed sulkily. " The chorus is believe it if ye like! "

" Go on," Aggie said. " What did she say?"

: " She said," Bell said. " She said: ' Do you know what's the cause of this war?' So I said no—though there's a lot o' things I could' a' mentioned—and do you know what she said? She said: 'Drink and gamblin'—that's what's the cause!'"

" Jesus Sufferin' Christ!" Meg cried.

" Ssh!" Aggie hissed. " Here's Nancy Pretty!"

As she bent over her ironing Nettie wondered what Jan was doing this afternoon. Was he on a route march? Had he been one of those who had waved to old Jessie? She didn't think he would have waved. Stanny would, of course! Stanny would not only have waved; he would have winked and called something. Stanny was fit for any climate. As for that fellow that Chrissie had been with . . . . . Nettie sighed, wondering if she should say anything about him to her mother.

Of course, Chrissie was able enough to look after herself. But. . . . . She'd see to-night when she was in alone with Ma. Jan was to be on guard-duty to-night, so she'd be able to stay in and wash her hair. Maybe if she got Ma in a good mood she'd sound her. . . . .

X.

On Saturday afternoon when Nettie met Jan he said: " We go long promenade in countree, Nettee. We take bus."

It had been raining all the previous night and during the forenoon, but now it was fair. The sky was clear and everything looked fresh. The whole countryside had an autumnal air. They said nothing as the bus slid past wet bronzed hedges. Jan's arm lay around Nettie's shoulders and his hand stroked the cloth of her sleeve. She looked out of the steamy window, content to nestle in the crook of his arm. Pale auburn fir-trees lined the road, their low-hanging branches striking the top of the bus, rustling on it like the light patter of machine-gun bullets. The sound sent little shivers down her spine, and she shrank closer to Jan.

They got off the bus at a little village about five miles from Blytheden. Jan pointed to the local pub and said: " We go in here." Nettie shook her head, saying: " Oh no, I couldnie." But Jan took her arm and led her into the bar-parlour.

The place was empty, but voices and laughter sounded from the public bar. Nettie stood in front of the fire and

warmed her hands, looking up at a spotty reproduction of
The Laughing Cavalier. On one wall there was a huge map
of Europe, and on another a red-faced man in a kilt smiled
as he held up a glass of whisky. Wet foot-prints criss-crossed
over the worn brown linoleum. Jan rang the bell, and they
sat down at one of the small tables. A plump girl with
black frizzy hair sticking out under a soiled servant's cap
came and leaned her hands on the table, waiting for their
order. "It's cauld the day, isn't it?" she said to Nettie.

Nettie nodded, smiling. She saw the girl eyeing Jan, and
she wondered whether there were any Polish soldiers
stationed in this village.

Jan leaned forward: "A drink, Nettee?"

She shook her head. "I'll just ha'e some tea."

"Tea for two?" the girl said.

"Tea for two," Jan said. "And a bottle of wine."

"Oh no," Nettie said.

But Jan nodded to the girl. She grinned and said
"Okay!" And she winked at Nettie as she took the jug
of water and the cigarette-tray off the table and gave it a
wipe. Nettie flushed, then she frowned. And she tried to
appear at her ease and to behave as though she were in the
habit of having bottles of wine ordered for her every day
while the girl fetched a cloth and spread it on the table.
She looked out of the window, past the aspidistra in the
pot with the crinkled pink paper round it. An old woman
wearing a rinking-cap and a bright jazzy overall came out
of the house opposite and shovelled up some horse's dung
off the street.

Nettie turned away, looking down at her hands and then
across at Jan. He smiled and whispered: "Are you happee,
Nettee?"

"Sure," she said, and she began to hum *Are You Happy
At Your Work?* Jan joined in, humming the tune. He
leaned his head on his hands, his knees gripped hers between
them under the table.

When the girl brought the wine he poured out two
glasses. He held up his and said something in Polish. Nettie
said: "Eh?" But he smiled and nodded at her glass, not
trying to explain what it was. Nettie sipped her wine,
looking at the door, afraid that somebody she knew would

39

come in. It would just be like Mrs. Baxter or some friend of hers to appear!

But nobody came in. The pub shut at three o'clock, and they heard the people in the bar go out. A few of them were most unwilling to go and they had a tussle with the black-haired servant who giggled and tried to push them out. "Wait till I see yer wife, Tam Patterson!" they heard her shout. "I'll tell her what kind o' man ye are!"

After tea Nettie and Jan sat in front of the fire and finished the wine. Nettie sat slumped in a horse-hair easy-chair, not wanting to move. The wine and the heat from the fire had made her sleepy. Jan sat on the arm of her chair, smoothing her hair and saying: "We go now. Nettee."

But every time he said it Nettie shook her head and said: "Just a minute. What's all yer hurry?" She did not want to leave the cosiness of the drab room. She felt safe and secure in it. Jan's face looming over her was indistinct. She felt vaguely afraid every time she looked up at him; the fire-light was glowing red on his high cheek-bones and making his glossy hair shine. There was something so terribly foreign about him!

At last he said: "We go now, Nettee." And he gripped her hands and pulled her out of the chair. She stood for a second, swaying slightly. God, I'm drunk, she thought, I'd better go to the w.c.

When she came back Jan had paid the bill. He was standing very large and dark in the gloom of the passage, his forage-cap set swaggeringly to the side of his head. The collar of his great-coat was turned up, throwing a shadow across his face. His teeth gleamed as he gripped her by the elbow and murmured: "We go now, eh?"

They walked slowly out of the village. Nettie felt un-steady on her feet, and she was glad of the support of Jan's arm. Huge lemon-tinged clouds were drifting across the sky, and others, like hillocks of pink snow, framed the horizon. Brassy gleams of sunset were shining through them, giving everything a cold, naked air. Nettie shivered suddenly and leaned closer to Jan. "Gosh, it's cauld after that fire," she said.

Outside the village Jan propelled her towards a gate leading into a stubbled field. "What are we goin' in here for?" she said.

But Jan grinned, saying nothing. He put his arm tightly around her waist, shutting the gate behind them with the other hand. Nettie picked her way carefully over the stubble, terrified that some of the long stubble-shoots would tear her silk stockings. They made their way along the side of a tall clipped hawthorn hedge until they came to a plank across a narrow stream. Beyond it lay a small wilderness of bramble-bushes and bracken.

A path led through the brambles into a disused quarry. Nettie walked in front of Jan, looking down fearfully at the bramble-shoots that whipped against her legs. She did not listen to Jan whispering behind her: "Lovelee, lovelee Nettee."

She looked about, suddenly terrified. But there was no sign of life anywhere. The village and the smoke from the chimneys had disappeared. Jan grabbed her suddenly from behind and pulled her against him. "Lovelee, lovelee," he murmured, kissing her almost savagely. Her body was drawn in against his, her limbs shaping themselves to the curves of his. For a moment she struggled. Then waves and waves of ecstasy swept over her; her legs trembled so much that she was glad of the support of his arms. Her inside seemed to be rushing up towards her throat, and she gasped for breath.

Suddenly he released her. She swayed, blind with wine and passion. She reached out to Jan, trying to steady herself. He was taking off his great-coat. He laughed as he spread it on a bank of stiff-fronded bracken which was the colour of milk coffee. And he said something in Polish, in a teasing voice, as he caught her hands and pulled her against him again.

"No, Jan!" she cried. "No! Somebody'll see us!"

But he pushed her down on the coat and began to pull at her skirt. And something made her cry: "Mind ma stockin's! They're gettin' scarce and I'll no' get a new pair in a hurry!"

41

XI.

Nettie hurried to her work on Monday morning, biting a roll as she clattered on her high heels in the direction of the laundry. Bell had called for her, but she had still been in her bed, unmindful of Ma's repeated shouts to get up. She sighed with relief when she saw the other girls still standing at the door, and she pushed the last half of roll into her mouth, wiping away the flour from her chin and cheeks as she joined them.

" Hello, Nettie! " Meg called. " Have ye been asked The Question yet? "

Nettie swallowed the last bit of roll and said: " The Question? What question? "

" Ach ye ken! " Meg giggled and nudged Aggie. " Ye dinnie need to pretend that ye're so dumb. "

" I dinnie ken what ye're talkin' aboot, " Nettie said. " What question? "

" Have you been asked? " Meg asked Bell.

Bell giggled. " Have I no'? "

" What did ye say? " Meg said eagerly.

" Oh, I gave him his answer. " Bell tossed her head. " I asked him what he thought I was. "

" What question is it? " Nettie asked.

" Ach, ye dinnie need to pretend ye're simple, " Meg said in an exasperated voice. " Ye ken fine what we're talkin' aboot. Did Jan ask ye if ye'd sleep wi' him? "

" Slee——" Nettie's mouth opened and stayed open.

" Ye dinnie need to kid ye're surprised, " Meg said sarcastically. " Everybody's been asked. A' the other lassies in the laundry. It's the first thing the Poles learn. Beautiful girlie, will you sleep wis me? " She laughed raucously. " By God, I gi'en Stanny his answer when he said that to me. We were standin' at the door and I was gettin' ready for a bit o' canoodlin' when he says: ' We make lof. No babies.' "

Bell started to giggle, but Meg looked at her and she shut up. " I soon babied him! " she cried. " I tellt him what I thought o' him. "

" Ay, ye did! " Bell jeered.

" Did I no'? " Meg said. " I soon sent him packin'. "

" Ay, for how long? He'll be back the night again wi' the same story. "

"Will he?" Meg snorted. "Don't you believe it. I sent him to hell."

"I dinnie believe it," Bell said.

"I'm tellin' you!"

Nettie and Bell looked at Meg in an unbelieving way, then they looked at each other, shaking their heads. Meg shook her hair back and put her hands on her hips belligerently. But the situation was saved by Aggie.

"Do ye ken what I heard?" She lowered her voice and looked around to see that nobody was listening.

"No." They leaned forward.

Aggie giggled nervously, then she opened her eyes widely and said in a shocked voice: "I heard that the hospital was fu' o' women that had had their tits ... that had had their tits chewed off by the Poles!"

She giggled again so that the last words were almost inaudible. The other three looked at each other.

"Ach away!" Nettie said. "I dinnie believe it."

"It's the gospel truth," Aggie said solemnly. "Betty Jamieson tellt me. She kens somebody that's a ward-maid."

"I quite believe it," Meg said. "Thae Poles are fit for anythin'."

Bell laughed. "Stanny didnie try that on wi' you, did he?"

"No bloody fear!" Meg picked up a pile of laundered sheets and began to carry them to the office. "It was bad enough wi'oot that. Can you imagine! He wanted me to go to his barrack-room where there's at least a dozen other fellies!"

XII.

That night Meg and Bell surprised Nettie by going to a meeting that Elsie McClure had arranged in the back-parlour of the Blytheden Temperance Hotel. A Trade Union organiser from Edinburgh was coming to speak to them. Elsie implored Nettie to come, too. But Nettie said: "I cannie. I'm goin' oot wi' Jan. Besides, I wouldnie be found dead in ony o' the hotels in Blytheden. Ma mother would kill me if she found oot."

"But it's a Temperance Hotel," Elsie said. "It's the only place we could get. A' the halls are fu' o' sodgers. Ye'll ha'e to come. We need yer vote."

"Well, I cannie help it. I've got a date and I'm no' breakin' it for ony auld Union meetin'. Surely to God ye can vote wi'oot me!"

"I suppose we'll ha'e to." Elsie sighed. "Still, I wish ye'd come. It doesnie show much interest after the man comin' a' this distance. I hope everybody's no' like you."

The meeting was a success, however. "Only you and Aggie werenie there," Meg said to Nettie the next morning. "Everybody was there. Even Maisie Forbes."

"Huh, ye'll be made up wi' that wee sneak," Nettie said. "Ten chances to yin she'll gang and clipe aboot it to auld Scott."

"I dinnie think so. She's as keen as onybody else aboot the Union."

"What did ye dae after the meetin' was ower?" Nettie asked.

"We went to Bert's." Meg sighed happily and leaned her elbows on her board. "Oh, we had a great time!"

"Ay, and ye'll ha'e a great time if Nancy Pretty comes in and finds ye like this!"

"She's doon in the wash-hoose the noo," Meg said. But she straightened up and pretended to be busy in case Miss Scott would come in unexpectedly. "We had a lovely time," she said.

"Had ye?" Nettie said.

"Ay." Meg was going to lean on her board again, but she changed her mind. "We met some fellies."

"What fellies? Stanny and Paul?"

"Stanny!" Meg sniffed. "No, a far nicer felly than him. A felly called Vladimir. Oh, he's lovely. Tall—he's taller than Jan—and he's got lovely wavy hair."

"Did he ask ye The Question?" Nettie asked slyly.

"Of course no," Meg said indignantly. "He's a gentleman. No' like that Stanny."

"Bell met an awfu' nice felly, too," she said. "Didn't ye. Bell?"

"Christ, did we no'!" Bell shimmied to show how happy she had been. "We had a great time. He's goin' to take me

44

to the picters the night. His name's Jan, too. It must be a common sort o' name in Poland."

"It means John," Meg said. "Vladimir tellt me. He speaks awfu' guid English. What aboot comin' wi' us the night, Nettie, and gi'in' that sleekit Jan the go-by? I never liked the felly onyway. Vladdy'll get yin o' his pals for ye."

"No thank you," Nettie said. "I'm not having anything to do with your riff-raff."

"Whae the hell are ye ca'in' riff-raff?" Meg cried snappishly. "They're far nicer fellies than that crowd we met the first night. We must ha'e been unlucky to ha'e met such a crowd o' buggers."

"Maybe that's what you think," Nettie said. "But I've got a different opinion. Just wait and see what this crowd turns oot to be like afore ye begin' to misca' the others."

XIII.

In the following weeks Meg and Bell and most of the other girls changed their escorts so often that Mrs. Baxter said: "It's a guid job there are twa thoosand Poles in the district at the rate they're gettin' through them!"

The girls were always meeting "awfu' nice fellies," but none of them ever went with them for more than two or three nights. Always a beautiful romance looked like beginning, then the girl would be asked The Question or she would take umbrage at something the soldier did or said. Only Aggie and Nettie remained faithful to the sergeant and Jan. Meg and Bell were always chaffing them, wondering when they were going to give them up. But Aggie just shook her head and said primly: "We're no' a' as flighty and as hard to please as you twa." As for Nettie, she had no time to think about anybody but Jan. He was everything to her: he filled her nights, and throughout the days she thought continually about him, not joining in the other girls' conversation or even listening to it. She had never imagined that she would ever feel like this about anybody. She was moving in a world where the war and everything connected with it was far away. Even when she was brought back to earth with a bump she always contrived to land softly. She had given up complaining about the blackout and about the other inconveniences that the war caused, and she would listen in a sort of daze to her mother saying: "Whae would ha'e thought eighteen months ago that we would come to the likes o' this? Creepin' aboot in the dark, feared to show a light. And gettin' yer butter and sugar rationed and havin' a' this bother aboot fillin' in ration-books. I never thought that folk would ha'e to put up wi' it."

To Nettie it was all like a gramophone record that she had heard dozens of times: something that she could almost repeat by heart. It was a background to her thoughts of Jan: a chorus that could be heard faintly but did not intrude. Jan was under the spotlight on her stage, and blackouts or guard-duties or field-manoeuvres could not take away from his brightness. She never thought beyond that coming evening or the next day. And when she was with him, his arms clasping her to him, even thought was wiped out. Only a warm sensuous emotion filled her, and the blackout was a welcome blanket.

Then one forenoon Aggie said that she had given up the sergeant. She was ironing a sheet at the time, and she said it with studied casualness. There was a minute's silence, then Bell cried:

"Let's see the teeth-marks!"

Nettie suspected that Aggie had been wanting to give up the sergeant for some time, but that she had been afraid in case she would not get another bloke in a hurry. But Aggie said in explanation: "Ach, I was fed up wi' him. He wasnie learnin' English fast enough for ma taste. It was an awfu' job tryin' to make him understand. I never knew what to say to him."

"That's right, Aggie," Meg said sympathetically. "There are plenty mair where he came frae, onyway."

"And he was aye wantin' to go and sit in auld Scott's parlour," Aggie whined. "God, I see enough o' Nancy Pretty through the day wi'oot wantin' to see her at nights, too."

At dinner-time Nettie told her mother and Mrs. Baxter about Aggie. "He seemed a nice-like felly too," Mrs. Baxter said. "I met them comin' oot the picters the other night and he was awfu' polite, clickin' his heels and holdin' the door open for me. My, what a grand smell o' scent was comin' off him!"

"The Poles are awfu' for scent," Ma said. "The lassie in the chemist's was tellin' me that they're aye buyin' eau-de-cologne. They cannie get enough to keep them a' goin'. She was wonderin' what they did wi' it; whether they put it in their baths or what."

"Maybe they drink it!" Mrs. Baxter chuckled.

"I dinnie ken," Ma said. "I'll ha'e to ask Jan the next time he's in."

"Are ye still goin' wi' him, Nettie?" asked Mrs. Baxter. "I thought ye would ha'e gi'en him the go-by long afore this."

"What for?"

"Well—" Mrs. Baxter laughed uneasily and looked away. "Are ye able to speak to him at a', Mrs. Douglas?" she said.

"Oh ay," Ma said. "He's learnin' English real quick. It's right funny to hear him sometimes."

"Is Chrissie still goin' wi' her yin?" Mrs. Baxter asked.

"Oh, Chrissie!" Ma laughed. "She's had a few through her hands by this time."

"That's the stuff!" Mrs. Baxter tittered. "My, if I was only young again masel' I'd show them a thing or two! I wouldnie see a lot o' the lassies nowadays in ma road." She got up, preparing to go. "Well, I'll ha'e to go and see aboot Andy's dinner. I got a nice bit o' steak. I've just got it to grill for him. Ta, ta, Nettie, tell yer felly I was askin' for him."

But it was another ten minutes before Mrs. Baxter left. Most of that time was spent in talking about Poles. "Ah well," she said as she finally went, "the Irish tattie-howkers 'll be comin' soon. They'll be the boys for them! They'll no' wait to be asked the Question! They'll ha'e the breeks offen thae Poles afore they can cough!"

"Ay, they're a rough lot, the tattie-howkers," Ma said as she shut the door behind her garrulous friend and fetched Nettie's pudding from the oven. "Are ye seein' Jan the night again?" she asked.

"Ay," Nettie said.

Ma poured herself a cup of tea. "Mrs. Baxter's a right inquisitive auld bitch," she said. "Fine she kent that you and Jan were still goin' thegither. I could bet that she kens every move ye make. She's aye ahint that curtain o' hers. There's no' much she misses."

Nettie said nothing; she poured herself a cup of tea and took a packet of Woodbines from her pocket. "It's high time ye stopped smokin'," Ma said. "They're gettin' that dear."

"Ach to hell," Nettie said. "I might as well enjoy masel' while I'm young."

"Well, I dinnie ken," Ma said, sipping her tea thoughtfully, not looking at Nettie. "I wish in a way ye were a bit mair like Chrissie. I'm no' sayin', mind ye, that I approve o' her goin' oot wi' a' thae different fellies, but—" She tilted up her cup and drained it.

"But what?" Nettie said.

"Well—" Her mother poured more water into the teapot and flung the dregs of her cup into the fire before refilling it. "Have ye thought aboot what's goin' to happen when the war's feenished?" she said slowly.

"What's to happen about what?" Nettie put her cigarette carefully on the ledge of the sink before beginning to tidy her hair at the mirror.

"Well, I mean, Jan's a Pole, after a'," Ma said. "He'll be goin' away back to Poland. I mean, it's no' like Aberdeen or Edinburgh or even London. Poland's hunders and hunders o' miles away. Have ye thought aboot it?"

"Ach, there's plenty o' time to think aboot that," Nettie said, putting her cigarette into her mouth and struggling into her coat, holding her head back to keep the smoke out of her eyes.

"Is there?" Ma said. "I dinnie ken aboot that. Ye're better to nip the thing in the bud afore it gets ower far. Ye couldnie expect yer father and me to come and see ye in Poland, and if ye had ony bairns. . . . . I mean, we wouldnie ken what they were sayin'. . . . ."

"Ach away!" Nettie said, drawing her belt tight and giving her shoulders a wriggle.

"I mean, Jan's a nice enough felly and a' that," Ma said. "And he's learnin' English no' bad, but—" She gave her large red hand a feeble wave. "I mean, ye'll ha'e to think aboot it."

"Aw, why worry?" Nettie said, opening the door.

48

"Somebody's got to worry," Ma insisted. "I'll ha'e to speak to yer faither aboot it. I'll see if he'll no' tackle Jan."

Nettie sucked her cigarette with exasperation as she hurried to her work. Ma had beat about the bush like that several times lately, hinting and wondering. Worrying her head about nothing. And making other folk worry too. She had tried not to think about it until now. But once started she found that she could not prevent herself from returning to it, wondering what would happen. . . . .

XIV.

That evening when Mr. Douglas was getting ready to go out, his wife said: "Where are ye goin'? Mind what I tellt ye. Ye cannie go oot just yet."

"Ach, can ye no' dae it yersel'?" he grumbled.

"No, it's your job," she said. "After a', you're her faither."

"A' right." He sighed and lowered himself into his easy-chair again. He sat and re-read *The News*, reading the births and marriages and deaths, a part of the paper he very seldom read. Nettie wondered for a moment what her mother had meant, but she was so busy getting ready for Jan that she did not have time to bother about her father being there. She was buttoning her grey-and-salmon-striped dress in the bedroom when she heard a knock and she called: "That'll be Jan! Will ye let him in, Dad?"

"Here, Chrissie," she said. "Gi'es a hand wi' thur buttons."

"Ach, I havenie time," Chrissie said, without looking up from carefully drawing on a pair of silk-stockings. "I've to meet Eduard at seven o'clock and I'm late already."

"Ay sir, it's cauld the night, isn't it?" Mr. Douglas said, bringing Jan into the kitchen.

"Veree cauld," Jan said. He clicked his heels and bowed to Mrs. Douglas. "'Ello! Veree cauld, yes?"

"Ay, it's cauld right enough," Ma said. She looked meaningly at her husband and said: "I'll awa' and gi'e Nettie a hand."

"Cigarette?" Jan held out his case to Mr. Douglas.

"Well, I'm no' a cigarette-smoker, sir," Mr. Douglas said.

"I like ma pipe best. Still, for company's sake like—" He sniffed the cigarette and peered at the writing on it. "Foreign! Grand smell it's got."

He took two or three puffs, blowing out the smoke without inhaling. He held the cigarette close to his face and peered at the tip from beneath his bushy grey eyebrows. He sniffed. "It's just like a cigar, sir!"

"Good?" Jan said.

"Ay, it's guid right enough." Mr. Douglas settled back in his chair and cleared his throat. "Well, Jan, the missus was—er—wonderin'..... Ay, she was sayin'..... It's right cauld the night, isn't it?"

"Yes," Jan said. "Veree cauld."

"What picters are ye bound for the night, sir?"

"Picters?" Jan said. "Ah, cinema! Veree good picter. *Grapes of Wrath.*"

"Oh ay, I saw the trailer last week." Mr. Douglas looked at the bedroom door, then he leaned back in his chair, his thumbs in the arm-holes of his waistcoat. "I dinnie think I'll bother goin' and seen' it. I doot it'll no' be in ma line. It's a picter aboot puir folk. It'll be gey drab like. We see enough o' that aboot oor ain doors wi'oot goin' to see it on the picters. I like somethin' that takes me oot o' masel'. Something aboot gangsters or night clubs like. Or a right guid cowboy. I used to like the auld cowboy picters. Ay sir, I did that. Tom Mix or Buck Jones. They fairly took ye oot o' yersel'. I was right sorry to see that Tom Mix was killed twa or three weeks ago. Puir man....."

Mr. Douglas took another puff of his cigarette and sighed. "I mind an awfu' guid picter I once saw him in. I mind the girl he was in love wi'—only she would ha'e nothin' to dae wi' him, him bein' just an ordinary ranch-hand like— well, she was tied to the railway and the express was comin' along hell for leather. But Tom heard aboot it in time, sir, and he just took one leap onto the back o' yon horse o' his— What did they ca' it again? It had a short name. It's just on the tip o' ma tongue, sir. Hey, ma!" he called. "What did ye ca' yon horse o' Tom Mix's?"

"I dinnie ken," Ma snapped, following Nettie into the kitchen. "D'ye think I can mind everythin'?"

"Tony," Nettie said to her father.

"Ay, that's it!" he cried. "Tony!"

"Are ye ready, Jan?" she asked.

"Yes, readee," he grinned.

"Ready, boys, ready!" Mr. Douglas said, putting on his cap. "I'll just come oot wi' ye. S'long, missus, I'll be back sometime."

XV.

Nettie did not enjoy *The Grapes Of Wrath*, though her reasons for doing so were different from those of her father. On the way to the cinema Jan told her that there was a chance that his regiment might be sent to Greece.

Greece. . . . . For the first time for a while she remembered that there was a war and what the war meant. She recalled all that she had heard on the wireless during the past few days about the fighting in Greece. God, and Jan was going there! She sat numb with terror. Not even Jan's rummaging fingers could arouse any emotion in her. She tried to get as close to him as she could, trying to thaw the stupor of her mind against the warmth of his body. But it was useless.

Desperately she tried to follow the story unfolding on the screen. But it meant nothing to her. They were just a lot of actors piled on top of an overloaded truck. Road 66. Oklahoma. Wyoming. Road 66. Apparently they were looking for work. Nettie wondered what all the fuss was about. Didn't they keep saying that they were going to sunny California where there were peaches and grapes and oranges? So what were they making all the fuss about? That old man and that old half-witted woman who wanted to go back. . . . What were they bothering about? What had they to do with her and Jan sitting there on plush seats watching them? It was just a picture. Henry Fonda was not somebody called Tom Joad who had been in prison; Henry Fonda was Henry Fonda the film star. Jane Darwell was Jane Darwell. They were just acting. At the end of every day while they were making the film they had put off those old clothes and got into their limousines and driven away to their million-dollar mansions where they had held frenzied parties. Nettie knew. She read the film weeklies. It was just another picture. Nothing to do with her and

Jan. But Greece had something to do with them. Greece. A name on a map. But it wasn't a name on a map any longer. People were getting killed there. Bombs were falling and people were being machine-gunned and shells were......

Suddenly Nettie was aware that something was wrong. The film had stopped. In less than a second the young fry in the cheap seats downstairs were hooting and whistling. Nettie sighed with exasperation. Could they not give the operator time to change the reel or whatever it was he was doing? They were terribly impatient. They always hooted like that whenever this happened; and it happened quite often.

But the film did not go on after a few seconds as it usually did. Instead the cinema manager came onto the platform in front of the screen. He began to speak. Nettie could not catch his first few words, then she made out that there was an air-raid alarm. " But the show will just go on, ladies and gentlemen......"

Was that all? She relaxed again, snuggling against Jan. But only for a second. A few people rose and went out. God almighty, she thought as she and Jan were forced to rise to allow an almost hysterical woman with two children to scramble past them, could folk not sit still? What was the use of going out? It was just an alarm! They were better sitting comfortably in the pictures than crowding in a shelter or crouching under a stair. That's what Ma would be doing the now. She would be away along at the toot to Mrs. Baxter's, and they'd both stand huddled in the close between the tenements for as long as the alarm lasted. She and Chrissie had gone with Ma twice, then they'd refused to go again. Catching their deaths of cold, they had said. If they were going to get killed they'd get killed sitting comfortably in their own house. All the same, alarms were an awful nuisance. You could never settle down to anything because you never knew when something really might happen. Not that anything had happened near Blytheden yet. It was only in London and Greece and places like that......

The film started again, but Nettie no longer made any attempt to follow it. She pressed against Jan, clutching his arm with her hands as if trying to keep him in her grasp always. He whispered endearments in Polish and broken English. Their heads were so close together that the woman behind them tapped their shoulders and complained, so they shifted to the back row. There they sat in a world of their own, a world far removed from trucks of harassed and starving people searching blindly for the work to give them the money to buy the food their starving bodies needed. Although they in their way were starving, too: as much driven and harassed as the people in the film. The Netties and Jans of this world are legion. It is because the Netties and Jans are like this that films like *The Grapes of Wrath* must be made to show why wars like this happen.

Nettie passed her hands over Jan's head, drawing her palms down his cheeks. Her mouth clung wetly to his, and there were tears on her cheeks.

Crash!

CRASH!

The walls of the picture-house shook. Two or three people screamed. Nettie dug her fingers into Jan. "What was that?" she whispered hoarsely. But she knew that the picture-house had been struck.

Jan laughed reassuringly, and he muttered: "Sit steel, Nettee."

Some people had risen, but most of them sat still. Some of those in uniform cried to the civilians to stop. Nettie felt her heart pounding. She looked up fearfully at the roof, expecting to see it fall in.

But nothing happened. She had never thought that it would take so long for a building to begin to crumble. "But—but—" she gasped to Jan.

"Two miles," he said. "Three miles away." And he held up three fingers and grinned.

She sighed with relief. One, two, three . . . . she began to count to herself, having heard that by the time you counted ten the bomber would be far enough away not to be dangerous. But after she had reached ten she was still shaking. She wondered where Ma was. Would she be all right? If, as Jan said, it was two or three miles away, then she'd be all right. But still she would have got a scare. . . . .

Those who wanted to go had gone, and the rest of the audience settled itself calmly to watch the film. But it was a while before Nettie's rigidity loosened. She leaned for a long time against Jan, her eyes closed, listening apprehensively. Would there be any more crashes?

But there was no sound except the soft drawling American voices of the actors. Gradually Nettie relaxed. And as she relaxed her thoughts returned again to Greece.....

" Let's go, Jan," she whispered. " I want to get oot o' here."

" Not wait for All Clear?" he said.

" No, let's get oot o' here."

She was surprised to see so many people about the streets. Searchlights were piercing the blackout like the golden ribs of a black fan. It was if some superhuman hand were wielding it, flirting it gently, blowing the puny humans here and there as it willed. Far up beyond the tips of the golden ribs there were aeroplanes dodging the shafts of light. They could hear the droning, but the planes were too far away to know how many there were of them. Two or two hundred.... Two ... or two hundred....?

She leaned against Jan and he put his arm more firmly around her. " It is okay, Nettee," he said. " No danger."

" Ay, that's all very well for you," she said. " You that's been at Warsaw. But it's ower near for ma taste."

" Okay," Jan said. " We go in here."

Nettie said nothing as he led her into the lounge of the Royal Hotel. She was too scared to think of what her mother would say. She sighed with relief as they got into the warm brightness and she slumped into a chair. " Oh God, this is fine! "

As she did so she noticed Jan clicking his heels and bowing to somebody. It was Stanislaus. He had a girl with him. A strange girl whom Nettie had never seen before, a girl who did not belong to Blytheden. Nettie knew that she must be one of the women who had followed the Polish soldiers there. She had bright peroxided hair tied with a clover-coloured bandeau, and she had very narrow plucked eyebrows. Stanislaus rose and clicked his heels, but he did not make any move to come near them. The girl looked at

Nettie over her clasped scarlet-nailed hands, and she curled her lips slightly.

Jan ordered two whiskies. " Oh, I couldnie," Nettie said. " What would Ma say?"

Jan pushed the glass towards her, grinning. " Good!" he said and he drank his own whisky at a gulp.

" Okay," Nettie said.

She made a face after she had taken a sip. " Ugh, it's no' guid."

But Jan pressed her to finish the drink. When she had done so, she shuddered. In a few minutes, however, she began to feel the better of it. Jan raised his eyebrows. " Nice?"

Nettie craned her neck, shifting her seat on the leather settee so that she could see herself better in the large mirror which had an advertisement for whisky written across it in red and gold letters. She patted her curls, wondering if she should bring out her powder-puff and flap-jack while that woman was sitting there with Stanny. It was just a Woolworths flapjack and her puff was needing a wash. She wished now that she had let Jan buy her one when he had stopped the other day before a jeweller's window and asked her if there was anything she would like.

" Excuse me," she said.

When she came back Jan was talking to Stanislaus in Polish. The blonde woman was twisting a ring around her finger and staring past them as if unaware of their conversation. Jan clicked his heels and came back to his seat beside Nettie on the settee. He called the waitress and ordered two more whiskies. This time Nettie did not make any fuss; nor did she shudder when she gulped down her drink. " Gimme a cigarette, Jan," she said.

She leaned back and watched the cigarette-smoke spiralling upwards. For a moment before it thinned and evaporated into the thick air, she thought it was like a giant cork-screw and that her mouth was the bottle-neck. Jan put his arm around her and drew her against him. She giggled and gave him a dunt with her elbow, but she did not draw back when he put his arm more tightly around her. " Still afraid, Nettee?" he said teasingly.

"No, but I wish it was a' ower," she said. "Ye cannie ca' yer life yer ain wi' this auld war."

She hummed a few bars of the song the wireless was playing: *Take Lessons From Madame Lasonga.*

"And if she fancies you the lessons are free," she sang to Jan, wriggling her shoulders and making eyes at him. She smiled across at the woman with Stanislaus.

"You will have to excuse me before we go to meet your friend," the woman said slowly in a loud voice to Stanislaus. "I will have to revarnish my nails."

"Nails?" Stanislaus said, winking.

She repeated the words, then she rose and went out, her hips swaying, glancing at herself in the mirror as she passed.

Stanny came over and talked to them; he ordered drinks. "Who's your girl-friend?" Nettie said, sipping her gin and lime.

"Girl-friend," Stanny said. "Jeanette."

"Jeanette MacDonald!" Nettie giggled, and she drank off the remainder of her drink at a gulp. "Is she nicer than Meg?"

Stanny shrugged. "Yes, veree nice. Good pal, yes, damned good pal."

Stanny clicked his heels and excused himself when the blonde returned. He said something in a low voice to her, but she shook her head. Stanny appeared to argue with her, then he put on his great-coat and forage-cap, looking at himself in the mirror. The woman stood with a half-smile on her face, eyeing Nettie. "When you go *chez moi* you must tell me," she said. "I am curious to know."

She turned and went out without looking at them, but Stanny clicked his heels and bowed; and Jan rose and bowed after them.

"Where does that tart come from, anyway?" Nettie said in a loud voice, and she drank off the drink that the waitress had just brought to her. "What a dyed-lookin' bitch!" She giggled and nestled against Jan. "Gimme another cigarette, darlin'."

A girl on the wireless was singing *There'll Come Another Day.* Nettie closed her eyes, listening to the words in a state of drunken sentimentality. *The clouds will vanish, True Love will banish dull care away.....* She opened her eyes;

the smoke was stinging her nose, and she ground the cigarette on the ash-tray. She saw Jan through a mist; his dark hair and gleaming eyes. Oh Jan, oh Jan, how you can love! *The world will glow with gold and glory, Soon we'll forget that skies were grey, And like a lovely fairy story, There'll come another day* . . . . . .

In hundreds of places in Britain young couples were sitting, listening to this promise of a better world. Listening as some of their parents had listened to the promise held out in the popular songs of twenty-five years before. None of them ever thought that for one couple for whom the world would glow with gold and glory a hundred couples would never live under any skies but skies of grey. Or if they thought about it, they imagined that *they* would be the fortunate couple.

> *A day to bring you joy and laughter,*
> *For when the night has passed away*
> *You'll find that joy follows after.*
> *There'll come another day* . . . .

" Will there?" Nettie wondered.

" Lovelee, lovelee Nettee," Jan whispered.

" Oh Jan!" she said, and she clutched him, straining him against her. " Oh Jan, I couldnie bear to let ye go now . . . . ."

> *And there together in sunny weather*
> *We'll wander hand in hand.* . . . . .

The windows of the lounge rattled suddenly. Gun-fire. " I doot they're no' away yet," a man said. " There must be mair to come."

XVI.

" Damn them and their auld air-raid," Meg said the following day. " It fair spoiled ma night. I'd just clicked wi' an Air Force felly in Bert's when the sirens went and he had to rush away to the aerodrome. God, I was right mad. I was fair lookin' forrit to a change frae thae Poles."

" Is that a' ye've got to worry aboot?" Aggie said mournfully. " Ye might ha'e been killed. The bombs fell at Armitage Toll."

" Well, what aboot it?" Meg said. " That's three miles oot the Dunesk Road."

"Ay, but another second and they might ha'e fallen right on top o' ye."

"Ah well, what aboot it?" Meg laughed. "I wouldnie ha'e needed to come to this dump this mornin'."

"I'm right fed up," she said later on. "I think I'll try to get a job in a munition works."

"Ye might as well wait to see whether we're goin' to get a rise," Bell said, looking round to see that Miss Scott wasn't within hearing. "Elsie McClure says the Union man has written to auld Scott."

"We should see on Friday then," Meg said. "When we get oor pay."

The girls spoke about nothing else all week. The subject completely ousted the war and the Poles. But Nettie could not speak about it; she had more important things on her mind. Her anxiety about Jan had been partly relieved when he told her that perhaps after all they would not be going to Greece as Poland was not at war with Italy. Nettie did not understand the complexities of International relationships, but even if she had she would not have paid any attention. Another, a more personal matter, had swept away her fears for Jan. It became more important to her than all the Greeks and Poles and Italians.

She was terror-stricken. Nothing like this had ever happened to her before. And by God, she vowed, if it came all right this time she'd see that it never happened again. She'd have no more to do with Jan. She wished to God she had never seen him, wished even that he had been killed at Warsaw. Oh, Christ, if it would just come.....

But by Friday it had not happened, and she was almost hysterical with fear. The other girls commented on her sullenness and bad-temper. "Ye'd think ye'd pee-ed on a bed o' nettles," Bell said. "Ye're that ill-natured."

If it hadn't been for that Nettie might have confided in either her or Meg; she was terrified to say anything to Chrissie or Ma.

On Friday evening Maisie Forbes said: "Miss Scott wants to see all you girls in the office before you go."

Miss Scott was sitting at her desk. She did not look up when the girls, their coats on, began to go into the office.

She stared at a letter she was holding. The girls whispered to each other, shuffling with embarrassment. One or two of the bolder spirits giggled as they came in, but they quickly stifled their giggling once they were in the midst of the solemn atmosphere. Nettie stood between Meg and Bell, wishing she was home. Either that or dead. Yes, she wished she was dead. . . . . .

If it didn't happen to-night she'd go and see the doctor tomorrow afternoon. She wouldn't go to their own doctor in case he said anything to Ma; she'd go to a doctor in Edinburgh. Jan wanted her to go into the country with him, but she wasn't going. She'd gone into the country once too often. She wasn't going to have any more to do with him. Maybe the doctor in Edinburgh would tell her what to do. She'd be able to speak to a stranger better than she would be able to speak to her own doctor. He wouldn't know her. She could quite easily buy a Woolworths ring. Maybe he'd send her to one of those places. If only she had the nerve she'd ask somebody. Maisie Forbes might know. They said that once she had been nearly away with it. . . . . .

" Is that them all?" Miss Scott said, looking up.

Maisie Forbes stood inside the door. " Yes."

" All right."

The girls looked at each other when Maisie turned the key in the lock and stood with her back against the door. " What the hell!" Meg muttered to Nettie.

But Nettie was staring at the floor. She couldn't ask Maisie Forbes after all. Maisie was such a clipe that the news would be all round the place in no time. Maisie would just love a chance like this to speak about her. Oh God, if only she knew some place in Edinburgh. . . . . .

Miss Scott put on her rimless glasses and said: " I have a letter here from a Mr. Edwards of Edinburgh. A Mr. John P. Edwards of Edinburgh," she said sarcastically, looking at the letter with disgust. " A Trade Union organiser. Apparently some of you youg ladies wish to forb yourselves into a Trade Union branch. I must say I thingk you might have cob to me about it. It's not quite the thingk for me to hear about id from an outsider."

The girls stood silent, shuffling with fear and embarrassment. Nettie went on staring at the floor. Christ, if anything happened to her, Ma would throw a fit......
  "I'll have no sabodage here," Miss Scott cried. "You
scub of the gudders! None of you dow when you're well
off. I subbose you all wand to go to Munidions and buy
fur coads and pianos. Don'd led me hear any of you com-
blaining again or——"
  "Now, ged out!"
  They moved in a cowed way, not looking at each other
or at Miss Scott. Those nearest the door turned quickly,
seeking escape. But Maisie Forbes took her time about un-
locking it. She handed them their pay-envelopes and they
slunk past her. Many of them broke into a run as soon as
they were outside.
  Nettie took her envelope in a daze. Her face was haggard
and her eyes were dull. Meg and Bell cleeked their arms
into hers as they went out into the blackout. None of the
girls were talking; there was only the sound of dozens of
pairs of high heels clattering on the pavement. The three
of them teetered along the pavement in silence for a few
seconds, supporting each other. Then when they were
safely out of hearing of anybody at the laundry-door, Meg
cried harshly:
  "The auld bugger!"
  As if it were a signal all the girls began to chatter, raging
and swearing. They quickly recovered their toughness in
the blackout. Nettie alone said nothing about Miss Scott's
refusal to treat them fairly, and she did not listen to what
Meg and Bell were saying on either side of her. She was
glad of their friendly support, for she could see nothing in
the blackout that surrounded her. She did not completely
understand whom Meg was raging about. But it might be
Jan. He was only one of the many people in the world
whom the expression fitted. She was done with him. Done.

XVII.

Nettie took her tea in silence. Chrissie and Ma were
talking about Mrs. Baxter who said that she had been
assaulted in the blackout. "She says it was a Pole," Ma
said. "But the Poles are no' that daft. They're no' goin' to

bother themsels pouncin' on onybody wi' a figger like hers."

"I dinnie believe she got pounced on at a'," Chrissie said.

"No, she's annoyed because she hasnie got pounced on—that's what's aggravatin' her," Ma said.

Nettie didn't listen to them. As soon as she had finished her tea she went down the garden to the dry closet. She struck three matches before she managed to light the candle. "Christ, what a life!" she muttered irritably, examining the blackout to see that it was all right. You might as well be dead. Oh God, if something didn't happen to-night she'd go crazy. One thing certain: she wasn't taking any more chances. She had finished with Jan. She wasn't going to meet him to-night. He could stand in the blackout and freeze to death for all she cared. . . . . . .

When she went back to the kitchen, her eyes were sparkling and she was singing *And when the shadows fall behind you there'll come another day.*

"Did you see your letter?" Ma asked, looking up from the sink.

"What letter?" Nettie said, pushing past Ma and arranging her curls before the mirror.

"There's a letter for ye on the mantelpiece. It came this afternoon. There's a lot o' foreign stamps on it."

Nettie took down the letter and looked curiously at it. She put it down on the table and put on her coat. She hummed as she rubbed some lipstick on her mouth. She looked at the clock, then she picked up the letter and opened it.

"Whae's it frae?" Ma said.

"Oh, it's a letter frae Harry Whatsisname," Nettie said, putting it back in the envelope and throwing it onto the dresser. "Pages and pages!" she said, buttoning her coat and making for the door. "I cannie be bothered readin' it the now. I havenie time. I must hurry up and meet Jan. Cheerio!"

October, 1940—New Year's Day, 1941.

61

2. THE CLOUDS ARE BIG
WITH MERCY

In the street there was a company of about thirty young
Requetes with red berets and green armlets with red crosses.
Their leader, a suave young officer on a grey horse, was
haranguing Jose's grandfather, old Alcalde Roya. The villagers were standing around, staring at the Requetes. Most
of the Requetes were young men; little older than boys, and
the hostile silence of the villagers overawed them. If it had
not been for their officer they would have marched on
quietly.

" The Generalissimo commands," the young officer was
shouting to the Alcalde.

Grandfather Roya spread out his hands and shrugged.

" There are no quarters unless you are willing to pay
for them," he said.

" In the name of the Generalissimo," the young officer
cried, swishing his whip through the air.

The Alcalde still shrugged imperviously.

" No payment, no quarters," he said.

" My men have guns," the officer said.

The Alcalde laughed. " We are poor unarmed people,"
he said.

Jose, watching to see the effect of this announcement, was amazed at his grandfather's courage. Every minute the little boy expected the officer to give the word of command, and he prepared to huddle down against the wall in readiness for a rain of bullets. But the officer seemed at a loss. Obviously he was afraid to give the order to fire. His men were raw and unaccustomed to their guns, and he had no idea what effect such an order would have on them. For although the peasants were hostile, they were, after all, people like the Requetes themselves.

But like most of his class, the young officer had an air of braggadocio that usually carried things off in the way he wanted them to be carried. He gave the order to fire.

Immediately the villagers disappeared from the street. There was no disorder in their departure; they drifted into their houses like icicles dissolving under a downpour of rain. And before they could make up their minds to obey their officer's command, the Requetes had nobody to fire at except a dirty-faced little boy, standing with a grin on his face and one arm out-flung in the Fascist salute.

Jose just got a glimpse of Manuel Uritia standing like this before Senora Roya caught him by the shoulder and hauled him into the house. And he hadn't time to think about it then; he was too busy helping Papa to barricade the door and the windows.

" Now! " Jose Maria Roya cried, flashing his teeth derisively. " Let them shoot! "

But the Requetes did not shoot. Jose did not know what happened next. His mother put him to bed and, valiantly though he strove to keep awake, he fell asleep.

The next morning he found that the Requetes had gone. He heard that they had spent the night at Fat Antonia's and that they had drunk most of her wine. Antonia had locked herself in an upper room, where she had had hysterics while the Requetes did what they liked with her property. Jose heard all this from Manuel, who boasted about the way the Fascists had made much of him.

Jose did not believe him. All that he believed, all that he cared to remember of that night was the picture of Manuel standing with his arm raised in the hated salute. It was burned on his brain as if burned by acid. Everything else that happened in the following weeks became jumbled in his memory: his brain was like a panoramic film on which was printed men marching, black-hatted Militia men and red-capped Carlists, men and horses, men and guns, men marching and marching ... and all these pictures followed so closely upon each other that he hadn't time to develop them into clear prints. Only the etching of Manuel remained crisp and outstanding. It was corroded deeply, something he would never forget.

*   *   *

A fly buzzed noisily on the schoolroom window. It reminded Jose of the noise the aeroplanes made when they flew over the village. The villagers were getting used to them now, but they had been scared the first time they flew over. They had not known whether they were Government planes or those of the insurgents. The first time they had belonged to Franco, and when they were over the village little black specks had dropped from them. And several houses had been knocked down and ten people killed. After that the villagers always ran out to the fields whenever they heard the planes coming. Sometimes though they came so quietly that they were over the village before anybody realized that they were there. Altogether thirty-one people had been killed or injured since the first planes flew over. Others had left since then. Most of the men had gone to fight. Women had taken their families and their belongings and set out for Madrid. Only those who were too old to travel or those who were injured or those who had no wish to leave their homes still remained.

But soon they, too, would have to go, Jose knew. Every day Franco's troops came nearer and nearer. Several times he had asked his mother if they would not set out for Madrid too. But always Senora Roya had shaken her head. "We shall stay here with the grandfather," she said. And she would look grimly in the direction where Franco's army lay, in the direction where her own man was fighting ... if he was still alive to fight. They did not know. They had not heard from him for weeks. But he was still alive, his wife assured herself a hundred times a day as she did her own work and his. He is still alive, she would exclaim joyously as the child she would soon bear made his presence felt in her womb.

Don Balthazar still taught in his little school, but every day his pupils diminished in numbers, and every day he found it more and more difficult to teach those who remained. They were learning so quickly these days, learning of things that he could not teach them. He sighed when he remembered the children in England where he had once lived: they did not mature so quickly. But he supposed these were abnormal times and that one should expect abnormal feelings. Though it was strange to think of these childish faces in front of him loving and hating like adults. He sighed again and looked down at the book that lay open on his desk. It was a book of poems in English by the poet, William Cowper. All his life Don Balthazar had been studying Cowper and planning that one day he would translate these poems into Spanish. But he had never had time to do so. Only in the last few weeks had he started in a desultory sort of way to prepare his text. But it was difficult with so many distractions. How could he manage to show the religious spirit and the peace in Cowper's poetry when the skies were raining death and destruction? Perhaps, he thought, it would be better to leave it until his retirement. A serene old age where he could mellow and muse upon the richness of Cowper's spirit. Peace and quiet ...

But would he ever get that? Any time now he might be stricken down by one of these bombs. He was no more immune than the illiterate peasant woman or her children. He sighed and looked down at his book ...

> Ye fearful saints, fresh courage take;
> The clouds ye so much dread
> Are big with mercy, and shall break
> In blessings on your head.

The clouds ye so much dread are big with mercy ... Nay, Señor Cowper, they are big with German and Italian planes. They shall break not with blessings but with bombs. Yet perhaps these bombs might be called blessings, he thought. There was so much misery in the world that perhaps those who got quickly out of it were to be envied.

He looked out of the window at the blue sky, a clear blue sky with faint white cloud-markings. He saw the rays of the sun. He heard the whistling of the birds. A butterfly flew past the shattered glass of the window.

It was better to be alive on such a day. One might have hunger and no home, no hopes and no friends, but there was still the blue sky and the sunshine. It was not a good day to think about death . . . Death was for the dark days, for the black brooding of a winter's night when you are shivering.

He looked over the ten pupils who were all that remained in his school. Their heads were bent over their books. He wondered what they were thinking about, wondered if they were absorbing the lesson or whether they were thinking of the army that was creeping nearer and nearer their homes every day . . .

Jose wondered if there would be another air-raid soon. He hoped so. He knew what he was going to do. He was going to kill Manuel. He was going to pay him back for giving the salute to the hated Requetes.

He had thought of it so often that every detail was clear in his head. All his plans were perfect. All that he needed now was the air-raid.

Once again he went over the course of action, lingering upon each tiny point, savouring every stroke with the joy of an artist. He resembled a bull-fighter goading the bull, taking a sadistic delight in cruelty for its own sake.

As soon as the alarm went he would keep close to Manuel. They would run, as they had always run hitherto, towards the hills at the back of the village. And as soon as they reached the rocky parts he would trip Manuel, and then, astride of his body, he would dash out Manuel's brains with heavy stones.

Jose's tongue flickered between his lips like the darting tongue of a snake. His eyes glinted as they pictured the scene. To have Manuel beneath him powerless, and to hear the crunching of the heavy boulders on his skull! That would be something to wipe out the memory of that hated salute! If only the air-raid would come now . . .

The fly buzzed, and somewhere in a nearby field a scythe swished. It was very hot, and Don Balthazar dozed over his translation of Cowper.

To-day? Jose wondered. Another raid was about due. The only difficulty would be to know to which side the planes belonged. For whenever they heard planes, all those who could do so ran to the shelter of the foothills, and from there they judged whether the planes belonged to friend or foe. It would never do if he killed Manuel and then discovered that the planes were Government planes. The whole success of his plan depended upon there being a great carnage.

Listening to the fly, as he re-plotted every detail, Jose suddenly became aware that the fly was making more noise than it should have done. He sat up straight and gave it all his attention. Yes, there was the whirring of the aeroplanes . . .

" The planes! " he cried.

Immediately there was pandemonium. The children forgot that they were in school under Don Balthazar's supervision. It was an air-raid, and in an air-raid it was every man for himself. They started for the door.

Don Balthazar roused himself from his contemplation of Cowper's spirit-healing words.

" Nonsense, Jose," he cried. " You are mistaken. There are no planes. Sit down, children."

For a moment he held the children back by the dignity of his office. And for a moment Jose thought that perhaps his imagination had got the better of his senses. Then with one rush the children swept past Don Balthazar and were out of the door before he could say any more. Grasping his books and papers, he followed them, his aging legs beginning to tremble already with excitement.

Looking towards the West he saw a cloud of aeroplanes drifting towards the village. They were still some distance off, but already he could see that they were bombers, the dreaded birds of destruction with death in their claws. For a moment he hesitated, then he hobbled towards the rope that was attached to the school-bell.

Dragging on it with all his strength he rang and rang as he had never rang before. All the time he watched the black specks creep nearer and nearer. He could see the silver of their wings shining: silver like the grin of a skull. Desperately he pulled and pulled at the rope . . .

* * *

Jose kept close to Manuel as they ran. He saw that the other boy was going to follow the rest of the children, so he cried: "This way, Manuel, this way!" And he veered off towards the path leading past Garcia's goat-hut to the gully he had chosen for his attack.

Manuel followed him. Jose kept ahead. They did not run too quickly; they were saving their breath for a final spurt. The planes were still some distance away. They could hear them plainly now, their engines booming, and above their sound they could hear the clanging of the bell. Presently Jose began to fall back, allowing Manuel to gain on him and then pass him. This suited his purpose. He kept within easy distance of the other boy. Looking up occasionally at the planes, he knew definitely that they were enemy planes. He whispered a short prayer of thanks to Jesus and the Virgin.

Past the goat-hut where the goats were grazing, they ran up the path to the copse of eucalyptus; through it, and they began to climb the rough-grassed slopes. Slithering and sliding they reached the top of the first foot-hill. "That way!" Jose cried, pointing to the gully. "They won't see us there."

He saw that the planes were circling over Puenta del Condad. The bell had stopped ringing, but he could hear shouts and screaming faintly beneath the whirring of the planes. The first bombs began to fall. He turned and ran after Manuel.

Now!

He looked round for a suitable boulder to begin with. Not too heavy, although it would need to be heavy enough to stun Manuel slightly. Ah, there was one . . .

In his eagerness to reach it, he stumbled and fell. Mother of God, this would have to happen! He tried to get up, but the pain in his knee made him cower back and cry with pain. He looked up and saw the planes taking wider and wider sweeps around the village.

" Manuel!" he screamed.

" What happened, Jose?" Manuel ran back to him.

Savagely Jose dug his teeth into his lips and tried to rise. But the effort was too much. Suddenly he became a little boy who needed his mother or somebody to pet him.

" My knee!" he whimpered. " Oh, my knee!"

Manuel bent down and examined it. " I don't think it's broken," he said calmly. He put his hands under Jose's armpits and raised him up. " If you lean on me I'll help you further up the gully," he said.

3. FOR THE HEATHEN

After the service the congregation stood in gossiping groups outside the church. Young Ronald Fyffe stood with two other Sunday School teachers to wait until it was time for Sunday School.

"It was a helluva sermon to-day, wasn't it?" Jim Mackenzie said.

"Damnable," Ronald said. "I thought the old piecan was never going to stop."

"He didn't worry me," Peter Robertson said. "I made up my line for tomorrow while he was droning."

"What are you backing in the two-thirty?" Jim said. "Firefly."

"No bloody good," Jim said. "Won't stay the course. I'm backing St. Oswald's Green."

"I fancy that, too," Ronald said. "Guess I'll have a couple of bob on it."

"There's old Davis looking out like an anxious mother," Jim said. "We'd better go in. He's afraid we've done a bunk and he'll need to take our classes himself."

They were moving towards the Church door when Mrs. Rutherford called to Ronald. She had her four-year-old son with her. "This is Eric's first day at Sunday School," she said. "Will you take him in your class to-day, Ronnie? Till he gets broken-in?"

"O.K." Ronald said.

He took Eric's hand and they were going in when Mrs. Rutherford called Ronald back to whisper final instructions. Ronald passed them on in a whisper to Eric. "Now, remember," he said. "Say that if you want to go."

"O.K. Toots!" Eric said.

I'll O.K. Toots you, Ronald thought, giving him a hymn-book and a shove into the pew beside his own class of boys between ten and eleven years of age. Tommy Beattie and Freddie Brown were sitting together and he made Eric sit between them, hoping this would prevent their usual Sunday fight. While waiting for Mr. Davis to stop speaking to Miss McMurtie the organist, Ronald marked his register. He had the names of a dozen boys in his class, but only five of them were here: Tommy and Freddie, and in the pew in front of them Alec Grey, John Gilzean and Sandy Ross, a tall shambling boy nick-named Carrotty.

"Were you at the match yesterday, Ronnie?" Tommy said.

"Uhuh. I'll tell you all about it later," Ronald said. "Old Davis is going to start."

The Superintendent gave out the first hymn, *I want to be like Jesus.*

Ronald put on his glasses and conscientiously got the place for Eric before he got it for himself. This hymn always reminded him of the calamity that had befallen him on his eleventh birthday in this same church. It was one of the tragedies of his youth: as tragic now, after seven years, as it had been then. Only now he saw the comic side, too, *although it's like laughing at a photograph you were so proud of when you got it taken but which you think now is the funniest thing: you realise that it must always have appeared funny to other people.*

It would never have happened if his birthday hadn't fallen on a Sunday. If it had been on a week-day he'd have gone to the nearest shop as soon as his Grandmother gave him the two-shilling piece. But since it was Sunday he put it in his trousers-pocket beside his penny for the collection. He'd have liked to keep the two coins separate, but there

71

was a hole in one of his pockets. While he was waiting for his parents to get ready for church he wondered what he would buy with the unexpected gift. A water-pistol, a pair of roller-skates, a cricket-bat, a fountain-pen: he wanted them all. He speculated about the supreme desirability of each of them in turn as he fingered the florin. He'd have liked to ask Dick's advice, but Granny had told him not to tell Dick as she had given him only a shilling for *his* birthday. He thought about it all the way to church. And sitting on the slippery wooden seat beside his mother he shifted uneasily as he put his hand in his pocket to make sure the florin was still there. He tried to catch Dick's eye, but Dick was sitting between their father and mother. Ronald sighed as he squirmed restlessly. *Why hadn't their pew a cushion like the Bakers'? Was it because Mr. Baker was an Elder?*

" Sit still, Ronnie," his mother hissed softly. " Look how good Dick is! "

Ronald sniffed because he had doubts about Dick's angelic appearance. He knew that Dick was studying the way the Rev. Mr. McGregor spoke in his soft Highland voice, saying *p* for *b*. But their mother didn't know that and she handed Ronald her handkerchief. He passed it politely over his nostrils and handed it back. The Rev. Mr. McGregor said that they would conclude the service by singing *I Want to be like Jesus,* after the collection was taken. And he reminded the congregation that the collection to-day was for the heathen, and he hoped that everybody would give liberally so that the heathen might be enabled to have nice churches where they could learn how much Jesus loved them. Ronald sighed as he passed the collection-bag to his mother, thinking that it was hard on the heathen to be forced to sit on hard wooden seats with no clothes. But on the way home he forgot about the heathen as he giggled helplessly at Dick imitating the minister announcing the hymn and saying: " Now, little poys and girls, rememper it iss petter to gif than to receive. Effery penny that you put in the pag to-day will enaple some little plack poy or girl to go to Sunday School and learn apout Shesus."

But Ronald hadn't laughed when he got home and discovered that he had put Granny's two-shilling piece in the bag instead of his penny for the collection.

Even yet, seven years later, he couldn't make up his mind as to whether he was angry at not having got the water-pistol or angry at having been the unwitting cause of twenty-four black boys having to go to church. Or was he most angry because he hadn't had the courage to ask for his florin back? What would he do if he made the same mistake now? And what would kids like Tommy Beattie or Freddie Brown do?

When the hymn ended Ronald noticed that Eric Rutherford was playing with a knife. "Where did you get that?" he said.

"I gave it to him," Tommy said. "It's O.K., Ronnie, he won't be able to open it. It takes me all my time; the blade's so stiff."

"Did you learn the last three verses of First Corinthians, chapter thirteen?" Ronald said. "You begin, Alec."

Alec had Faith and he managed to say the first verse. John had Hope, and with Ronald's help, he managed to stumble through the second verse. But Sandy had neither Faith nor Hope and he stood and gaped. So Ronald had Charity, although he could not resist the chance to gibe at Sandy's nick-name.

"And now abideth Faith, Hope and Carrotty—these three, but the greatest of these is Carrotty!"

The class laughed dutifully.

"Open your Bibles at St. Mark, chapter three," Ronald said.

"Aw, Ronnie!" Tommy said. "I thought you said you were goin' to tell us about the match?"

"So I am," Ronald said. "Only you'd better have your Bibles open in case Old Davis comes snooping around."

"My big billy says it was a rotten match," Freddie said.

"Your big billy's nuts," Tommy said. "He's like you."

"He is not. Gee, I wouldn't have a big billy like yours for anything. He was the biggest sap in the Boys Brigade."

"How do you know?" Tommy said. "You were never in the B.Bs."

"I was so. I was in the Cubs and then I was in the Life Boys and then I was in the B.Bs., then in the Scouts, then I went back to the B.Bs. That's my history. The only thing I haven't been is a Brownie."

"Maybe you'll be a fairy, yet!" Tommy said.

"Quit quarrellin'," Ronald said. "Here, stop it!" he cried to Eric, who was hacking the edge of the pew with Tommy's knife. "I knew that would happen," he said, taking the knife from him. "Keep an eye on him, you two, and kid you're reading your Bibles till I come back."

He went across to Jim Mackenzie and they whispered about form at Kempton Park the following day. The Rev. Mr. McGregor came in from the vestry. He stood inside the door and beamed as benevolently as he could on account of nature having endowed him with a face like an asthmatic ape. At once Mr. Davis became very busy. He stopped chaffing Miss McMurtie and began to go around the classes.

"Hey, Ronnie!" little Eric cried suddenly. "Are there any lavatories here?"

Mr. Davis was as surprised as if a horse had kicked him in the pants, and he catapulted towards Eric. "Here, here, my little man," he cried. "You mustn't call your teacher Ronnie. You must call him Mr. Fyffe."

He turned to Ronald and said irritably: "What's that little boy doing in your class, Fyffe?"

Ronald explained.

"Take him down to my son's class at once," Mr. Davis said. "It's pure nonsense. Coddling the boy."

Ronald led Eric to young George Davis's class of little boys and deposited him as thankfully as he would have deposited a sackful of rotten eggs. "You're welcome to him," he said, smiling sweetly at George, whom he disliked.

Mr. McGregor mounted the pulpit and began his usual Sunday School sermon. Ronald yawned and leaned back. He was fed up being a Sunday School teacher (it was ruining his reputation!) and he wondered what would be the best way to get out of it. He wished he'd as much courage as Dick. For that day the minister came to their home and asked them to be Sunday School teachers Dick had said: "No bloomin' fear. I've had enough of the church and Sunday School in my young life." Their parents had been as

horrified as the minister, but they hadn't dared say anything
to Dick, who had a mind of his own and didn't mind showing it. But they took it for granted that Ronald would do
what the Rev. Mr. McGregor wanted. Ronald was such
a nice boy! And weakly, of course, Ronald had done what
they expected of him. *You mug not to ask that two bob
back. That's symbolic. You'll always be like that. Afraid
to speak your mind in case people are annoyed.*

"The collection to-day will pe for the heathen," Mr.
McGregor said. "Now, little poys and girls, rememper that
it iss petter to gif than to receive. Effery penny that you
put in the pag to-day will enaple some little plack poy or
girl to go to Sunday School and learn apout Shesus."

It's a pity that you can't make the same mistake twice,
Ronald thought. How he'd love to march into the vestry
at the end of the service and ask if he could have his money
back!

He grinned suddenly. Why not? It would be a good
chance to have a row with old McGregor and old Davis, a
good excuse to stop being a Sunday School teacher. He'd
back them instead of St. Oswald's Green!

"All the little boys will now stand," Mr. Davis said.

There was a scrunching and a sighing like the noise of
the sea swishing the pebbles on the shore as all the little
boys stood to sing while the collection was being taken.
Only little Eric didn't rise.

"Now, now, my little man!" Mr. Davis said. "Stand up
with the other little boys."

"I'm not a little boy," Eric said huffily. "I'm a big boy."

But he stood when George Davis smiled nicely at him and
gripped him firmly by the arm. And he stood with his
mouth in a sullen pout while the other little boys sang
Shall We Gather At The River. Thank God, I'll never
hear that again, Ronald said to himself as he dropped a
florin in the collection-bag before passing it along to Tommy
Beattie.

At the end of the first verse Mr. Davis said: "Can't you
sing, little man?"

"No," Eric said.

"But surely you've heard the little birds sing?"

"I'm not a little bird," Eric said.

75

When the Sunday School finished, Ronald went into the vestry. Young George Davis was counting the collection. Ronald was sorry that Mr. Davis and Mr. McGregor weren't there.

"Oh, George," he said. "I put a two-shilling piece in the bag by mistake. I wonder if I could have it back?"

He waited for George to call for his father or the minister. But George didn't move. He smiled affably with his yellowish buck-teeth, and he indicated the piles of pennies and halfpennies.

"You must be making a mistake, Ronnie," he said. "There's no two-shilling piece here."

4. WASHED IN THE BLOOD

I remember that once I wanted to be saved. When I was a little girl a black Revivalist came to our village and converted a lot of the villagers. He had a tent pitched on the village-green, and every night he stood outside it and cried to everybody to come and be washed in the blood of the lamb. Always he drew a crowd around him; partly because most of them had nothing better to do, and partly because his blackness was strange. We children especially never got tired of gaping at his shiny black face; his strangeness seemed to us something desirable and romantic.

The men who stood and gossiped and smoked every night at the bridge used to laugh when the Nigger came and began his oration. "Ay, man," they would cry. "How many souls have ye saved the day? Has another auld wife got doon on her knees and seen the light?" But the Nigger never took any notice of them. He grinned and stood on top of a box outside his tent, which was plastered with Biblical messages, and he would begin to deliver his message to suffering humanity. And soon the inevitable crowd would gather around him, even the men at the bridge gradually drawing nearer in a sheepish fashion. "Just in case we miss onythin' guid," they would remark to each other in excuse.

Only one of them always remained seated on the wall of the bridge, and that was Nessie McEndrick's father. Jamie McEndrick never moved from his seat. He puffed at his clay pipe and spat occasionally into the greenish-brown water far beneath him. He was the village joiner and carpenter, a big stout man with a brosey red face. He always sat still, his blue-striped shirt showing between his unbuttoned waistcoat and the bulging top of his trousers, and when he was very drunk he would cry out things about the Nigger and the Polar. I didn't know what he meant then, but I would know now.

The Polar was Mrs. Campbell who cleaned the school and kept lodgers. She was a widow, a huge stout shapeless woman with dirty white hair screwed into a bun on top of her head. She was usually dressed in a dirty whitish-grey overall, and it was this overall that had earned her the name of the Polar. Somebody had seen her bending down one day and had remarked that she looked like a big dirty Polar bear, and the name had stuck.

Besides keeping lodgers and cleaning the school, the Polar had a Cyclists' Rest. There was a crudely-printed notice on a board beside her door: CYCLISTS REST. TEA AND REFRESHMENTS. The Polar was tireless in finding ways to make enough to keep herself and her family. They were a shiftless lot. There was Willie the Polar, who was two classes ahead of me at school. He was supposed to be half daft; though, as some people said, " You would have a job touching the daft bit!" Occasionally the Polar's Soldier came home. He was a fine looking young man who had served in the Boer War and had elected to remain in the army. He was the only one of the Polar's family about whom I ever heard my mother say a good word. I had a school-girlish crush on him. He was tall and, in my young and inexperienced eyes, romantic-looking. I daresay that if I'd been older I wouldn't have given him a second thought. If I saw him now I'd probably think him common. But then I spent a lot of time thinking about him, and for years I kept a post-card that he once sent me—why. God alone knows, because he hardly ever had taken notice of me in the village, and his family and mine were not on what you'd call speaking terms. It was a gaudily coloured view of Salisbury Plain, and on it was written: "Here on manoeuvres for two weeks. Hope you are well. I am in the pink. Your friend, B. Campbell." Lastly there was Bella the Polar, a gawky girl in her teens. She was in service, but she was more often at home between jobs than she was employed. She didn't seem able to keep jobs. "And no wonder!" my mother said. "Who would keep a slut like that in their kitchen? But what else could you expect with a mother like that?"

My mother never spoke to the Polar, and she would not have dreamed of eating anything out of the Polar's house. I remember that once the Polar made toffee, and Willie the Polar canvassed for orders at the school. Everybody was buying it—out of pity, I suppose, for the Polar's penury—and I wanted to be upsides with everybody else; I hated to be different from the other children. I begged my mother to buy some, but she wouldn't. "I'll toffee you!" she said. "I wouldn't eat one mouthful that came out of that woman's house."

My mother was what was called a bit uppish in the village, and she had few friends. Not that she saw the need to have any. She had her husband and her children to look after, and she was satisfied with doing that. She said that she hadn't any time for Revivalist meetings and nonsense like that.

During the short time he stayed with her, the Nigger was the Polar's favourite lodger. It was the Polar who first gave us children a row for calling him the Nigger.

"Ye should be ashamed o' yersels," she said. "Cryin' decent folk names like that. If I hear ony o' ye callin' him onythin' but Mr. Abdul after this, I'll sort ye."

It was the Polar who learned that Mr. Abdul came from Abyssinia. "It's just ower the hill frae Egypt," she explained to somebody. "He says that he's goin' to take oor Willie back wi' him when he goes. Oor Willie's awfu' keen to be a missionary."

I heard Jamie McEndrick say that the Polar had learned lots of other things about the Nigger besides this, but when I asked my mother what sort of things, she told me not to be inquisitive. "Bairns should be seen and not heard," she said.

79

We children used to crowd around Mr. Abdul every night and listen to his exhortations, and it wasn't long until nearly every child in the village was saved. Every one of them wanted to go with him to Abyssinia to be a missionary like Willie the Polar. We were all sure that we would be much better missionaries than him.

Pretty soon everybody was saved except me and my little brother, Archie. We would have been saved, too, only our mother wouldn't let us. She forbade us even to go near the mission tent.

I pleaded and argued with her. "Why can't I be saved?" I asked. "Everybody else is getting saved but me. Lizzie Macdonald and Bessie Simpson and Nessie McEndrick—everybody in my class is getting saved. Even Murdo Anderson, and you know how wild he is. Why can't I get saved, too?"

"Because you can't, that's all," my mother would say. "Now, get out of here and don't let me hear any more about it. Away along to Mrs. Irving's and get me five pounds of sugar and a bar of yellow soap."

But nothing that my mother said could damp me. I saw how happy all the other children were after they had been saved, and I wanted to join them in their happiness. They still looked the same as usual, but I knew they couldn't be the same. Inside they must be different. Only something wonderful inside them could make them pray and sing like that inside the tent every night. None of them had ever prayed and sung in the same way in the drab Parish Church. Except Murdo Anderson, and he had always been up to some mischief under the book-board in the Anderson pew in the gallery. All the others, however, had always been quiet and frightened-looking. But here around the Nigger, warmed by his wide grin and ever-spread arms, they leaped and shouted joyfully, frisking like the new-born lambs the Nigger said they were. And the more they frisked and sang the more deeply I wanted to frisk and sing with them. I felt like a pariah, out in the cold.

And so, although my mother had forbidden it, I used to sneak out of the house every night and go down to the green. I hovered about the outskirts of the crowd around the door of the tent, and above their heads and shoulders I could see Mr. Abdul's face, grinning and sweating with love and tenderness. The sight of it heartened me and made me forget my fears of being found out. " Come unto Jesus all ye who labour and are cast down," he would cry. And under the soothing magic of his voice, impelled by his wild dark eyes, those sedate Scottish ploughmen and villagers, the product of generations of Calvinism, would cry " Hallelujah!" and get down on their knees, moaning and recounting their sins. And then they would enter the tent: accepted into the bosom of the Lord. They were the Elect, and I wanted passionately to be one of them. I wanted to enter the tent, too, to become part of the mass; to think as they did, to do what they did, and to have the same emotions at the same time.

Almost the entire village was soon filled with an air of religious ecstasy, and people were going about calling each other Brother and Sister.

Our household was one of the few that was not saved. My mother rigidly set her lips against it. " A lot of havers," she said. " As if the auld Scottish kirk and the Reverend Mr. McIver wasn't guid enough for most o' them."

The Rev. Mr. McIver also had something to say about it. He saw his congregation growing smaller and smaller every Sunday. " Something must be done about it," he said to my father who was one of the chief elders.

" Ay, but what?" My father began to scratch his head, but he stopped when he remembered that he was speaking to the minister. " It's no' as if it was a heathen religion he was teachin' them."

" That's right." Mr. McIver tapped his thin lips with the tips of his soft white fingers. " It's not as if it were Buddhism or Mohammedanism or any of those new-fangled things......"

The Rev. Mr. McIver began to come to our house often after this, and he and my father would sit and talk in low voices in the front parlour, stopping their conversation whenever anybody went near the door. My mother warned my brother and me that we were not to go in. " Out ye go and play," she would say.

This I was always glad to do. And gradually I would play farther and farther away from the house, until when I thought I was far enough out of sight and hearing, I would make for the village-green. And when I got there I would skulk around the outside of the tent, listening to the joyous Hallelujahs and Hosannas that sounded from within. All the time, although I wanted desperately to creep in, too, I was terrified to do so in case some woman like ourselves who was not saved and who remained faithful to Mr. McIver's preaching might tell my mother that I was one of the Nigger's followers. It was galling to remain outside the tent, but much as I wanted to become part of the swaying and singing mass inside, my fear of my mother was stronger than any pleasure I might have obtained from it. And so I remained near the bridge, and I often overheard Jamie McEndrick's drunken remarks about the Nigger and the Polar.

Of all the men who had been in the habit of gathering at the bridge after they came out of the pub, Jamie McEndrick alone remained. They said that he was almost the only customer the publican had left; the Nigger had saved the others. But as if to make up for the others' default, Jamie drank more than ever. Many a night my attention wandered between the sounds that came from the tent and the antics and roars of the drunk man. I used to shiver in the darkness, knowing that I should have been home and in bed long before, knowing that I would get a row for being out so late, and yet afraid to move, fascinated by the two rival attractions. Often he nearly fell over the bridge when he got caught in a drunken frenzy of denunciation against Mr. Abdul and his prophetic teaching. I began to dislike Jamie very much; I felt that he was an evil man, and I wouldn't have been sorry if he had fallen into the burn. It seemed to my childlike mind that the tent and he represented good and evil, and I passionately wanted the evil to be exterminated, even though it was just in the person of the drunken joiner. I realize now that this was a thought of which Mr. Abdul probably would not have approved.

After Mr. Abdul had been in the village a few weeks and had converted everybody but a few faithful Auld Kirkers, the Polar started a Sunday School for those children who were saved. I see now that religious fervour alone could not have accounted for this; the Polar always had an eye to money-making. Though what money she could have made out of her Sunday School I cannot imagine.

I urged my mother to allow my brother and me to go. "Everybody's going to it," I said. "All the girls in my class are going. Bessie Simpson and Nessie McEndrick....."

"Nessie McEndrick?" my mother said. "Her father should be ashamed of himself."

"Can I go?" I pleaded.

".No, you can't go," she said. "And that's final."

There were only a few children remaining at the Parish Church Sunday School, and it seemed a dull place compared with what I heard about the Polar's Sunday School. She held it in her parlour, and the children sang while the Polar pounded hymns on her wheezy old organ. Murdo Anderson boasted to everybody that he had been allowed to play the organ and that Mr. Abdul had given him his blessing. "I'm maybe goin' to Abyssinia to be a missionary, too," he said. "I'd be a better missionary than Willie the Polar." This made me more passionately anxious to go, but no matter what I did to please my mother she would not allow me to go.

Archie wanted to go, too; he was as keen to be saved as I was, but for different reasons. He wanted to go to Abyssinia with Murdo Anderson and Willie the Polar. "But we'll get rid o' daft Willie quick," he said. "I hope a tiger eats him." He talked a lot about the elephants and lions he was going to shoot. It never seemed to occur to him that being a missionary was something quite different. But this had occurred to me. I wanted to nurse the little black children and pray for their souls; I wanted to pray that they would never be unhappy and outcasts as I was an outcast at that time. I wanted them to bask in the radiance of Mr. Abdul's smile and to sing hosannas with the other children. That I was apart from the others at that moment did not matter; I knew it was only temporary. I knew that soon I would be one of them. I would be saved and I would go with Mr. Abdul to Abyssinia to be a missionary. I knew it would be a hard life, a precarious life, and that I might never see my mother and father again. But that did not matter. I would be a missionary and I would do good. Archie, however, though he was keen to be a missionary, too, did not seem to think of the dangers and hardships. Apparently his immediate desire was to go to the Sunday School because he heard from the other boys that the Polar gave them sweeties to eat between hymns.

But our mother said: " Enough of this nonsense. You're not going one foot. I dare you to step inside that woman's dirty house."

Finally Archie made the awful suggestion. " We'll skip our own Sunday School," he said, " and we'll go to the Polar's."

I was horrified, but not as horrified as I should have been. For the same idea had struck me, though I had been too afraid to mention it to Archie.

The following Sunday when we came out of the Kirk, we stayed behind as usual in the church-yard, and our parents left us. " Have you got your halfpennies for the bag?" my mother said, although she knew quite well that we had. But it was a question that she asked every Sunday, a sort of ritual, every bit as important as the actual going to Kirk and Sunday School.

We nodded.

" And have ye got a clean hankie, Archie?" she said. " See that he keeps his nose clean, Thomasina."

" Yes, mother," I said.

We stood besides old Sandy Irving's grave and we waited until they were out of sight, my mother's long black skirt sending the dust up over my father's highly-polished black boots and narrow trousers. While we waited, we traced our fingers over the lettering on the new granite stone. *Sacred to the Memory of Alexander Ramsay Irving. Born 3rd July 1820. Died 4th April, 1905.*

" Now," Archie whispered.

We looked to see that neither the beadle nor the minister were at the kirk door and that none of the small congregation still standing about in groups were watching us; and we ran across the churchyard and climbed the style that led into Ned Purdie's orchard. We skirted through it, watching warily for Ned or his old dog, Snatcher. I was terrified of Snatcher, but I was so anxious to be saved that I would have dared a dozen Snatchers in order to go to the Polar's Sunday School.

We were almost out of the orchard when we heard a bark. "Come on!" Archie cried, and he grabbed my hand and hauled me after him. I clutched my muff and prayed that I wouldn't let it fall. It was a white ermine muff that I had got from my Aunt Minnie and I was very proud of it because none of the other girls had muffs. The branch of a tree caught my large white leghorn hat and whipped it off my head, but the elastic band under my chin held it. I was so terrified of Snatcher and so intent upon running that I didn't feel any pain when the elastic nipped into my throat. "Quick, Ina!" Archie gasped. "Through here."

We scrambled through the hedge. My long curls that my mother had twisted so patiently into curl-papers the evening before got caught in the hawthorn, but I jerked them loose. My ribbon was dangling; I tore it off in case it would fall. I panted across the field after Archie.

"We're all right now," he said.

We leaned against the gable of an old stable, breathless with our exertions. "You should see yourself, Ina," Archie grinned. "You aren't half a sight! "

"You're a sight yourself," I said.

We tidied each other's clothes, then we began to walk sedately towards the Polar's, going the back way and keeping careful watch in case anybody saw us. As we edged round the Polar's house we heard the sound of singing and the pealing of the organ.

"We're late," I whispered. "It's started."

Archie tugged my skirt and whispered: "Let's look in the window first."

I held his hand and we peered in the parlour window. I saw Murdo Anderson bawling loudly, a beatific look on his snub-nosed face. The Nigger was playing the organ, and the Polar was standing in the middle of the floor. Her arms were held wide and she lifted them up and down as she led the singing:

" Are you washed? Are you washed? Are you washed in the blood of the lamb?"

I closed my eyes and swayed with the rhythm. This was what I wanted: this being part of a crowd, all feeling the same emotion at the same time. I moved towards the door, eager to get inside and to become even more welded into the mass. I put out my hand for Archie, but he drew back.

He tittered, and then to my horror he began to sway his arms, imitating the Polar. And he twisted his face into a caricature of hers. " Are you washed . . .?" He couldn't sing for giggling.

I made a dive at him, but he drew back, and then when I clenched my fists, he ran away laughing. I ran after him, but he was faster than I was. I had already run so much and my high black lacing-boots were hurting me so much that I couldn't make up on him. I was furious. He was making a mock of something that I knew to be precious and holy.

I went back to the window, but my tears of rage clouded my vision. I pressed my face against the pane, realizing dimly that more than the glass separated me from the joyous crowd inside. I wanted deperately to go inside, but I hadn't the courage to go without Archie. It was galling to remain outside, an outcast.

I sank my teeth into my lips to keep me from crying aloud at the sight of their happy faces. The singing stopped and they left their places and crowded around the Polar. She engulfed as many of them as she could in her outspread arms. I heard cries of " Tell us a story, Mrs. Campbell." I strained my ears, afraid I would miss anything, and I watched them enviously. Mr. Abdul was sitting at the organ, smiling at them all, his hands lying loosely on the keys. I ached to stand beside him, to have him put his hand in blessing on my head. And I wished passionately that I could become clean and saint-like like him and go with him when he went back to Abyssinia.

" Tell us a story, Mrs. Campbell!" The cry came from all corners of the room, and the Polar smiled and nodded at them. I pressed myself against the window, trying to warm myself from her love through the dirty glass. I wished that her arm was around me as it was around Nessie McEndrick.

The Polar closed her eyes and held her face up to the ceiling as if praying for divine guidance. The children watched eagerly, their eyes wide with expectation.

"The Lord Jesus was a carpenter," she cried. "He was the son of a carpenter, and he became a carpenter himself, just like—just like little Nessie McEndrick's father....."

I stood back, horrified. I remembered the things that I had heard Jamie McEndrick say at the bridge. And slowly I turned and went home. I no longer wanted to be saved. And I've never wanted to be saved since.

5. THE LOONY

Miss Mayfield would never have considered the job if she hadn't been trying to escape from the clutches of the Dole. That was the villain with the black moustache who cried " Curses ! " and assailed not her virtue but her pride. It was not that she minded drawing money from the Unemployment Exchange; after over thirty years of hard work she felt that it was no more than her due. But it was the public way in which she had to apply for relief to which she objected. She came in contact with such frightful people—especially among the officials.

" Simply terrible folk," she said to Mrs. Spowart, the cook. " Really, I never thought there were such folk till I first went to the Dole."

" It takes a' kinds to make a world," said Mrs. Spowart. " And shairly they couldnie ha'e been ony mair funny than puir Miss Rhona."

" Well, that's right," agreed Miss Mayfield, for Miss Rhona was indeed much queerer than anybody she had seen at the Unemployment Exchange. When Mr. Rattray, the lawyer, had engaged her as companion for Miss Rhona, he had said : " Er—of course, you must understand, Miss—er— Mayfield, that you will need to be rather more than a companion. Miss Rhona is—er—mentally deficient."

"And that's putting it mildly," said Miss Mayfield to the cook. "Mentally deficient! Gee whiz, she's fair loony!"

Miss Rhona was thirty-four, according to her birth-certificate, but she hadn't developed physically since she was seven or eight. And she hadn't developed mentally since she was a baby. If she had developed mentally at all.

All day Miss Rhona sat behind the lace curtains at the drawing-room window and gazed out at the street. Her hands lay listlessly in her lap. Passers-by who happened to look up always took a second glance at the big pumpkin-shaped head and the flat yellowish face. And children of the neighbourhood often came and stood on the pavement, putting out their tongues and calling: "Yah, funny face, whae's got a face like a suet-pudden?" until either Miss Mayfield or Mrs. Spowart drove them away.

All day Miss Rhona sat in her rocking-chair and rocked. That was the only movement she ever made. Rock, rock, rock—backward and forward the chair would go until it began to get on Miss Mayfield's nerves.

Although Miss Mayfield always called her the Loony when speaking of her to Mrs. Spowart or other friends, Miss Rhona showed no vestiges of that drooling imbecility which characterises so many half-wits. There were no mouthings or epileptic fits, no weird, unearthly yells, no twitchings of her misshapen body. Instead there was a calmness more terrifying in a way than any half-murderous attack would have been. Miss Mayfield often said: "If she'd throw something at me or yell or roll on the floor, I'd know where I was. But she's so quiet, sitting there all day, doing nohing, not even twiddling her thumbs. Just rocking and rocking. She fair gives me the creeps. She never looks at me, but no matter where I am I can't help feeling that she's there. You know, I'm beginning to get feared of her."

At first Miss Mayfield did not find her work exacting. It was much more pleasant to wait upon the imbecile woman than to stand behind a counter and serve people as stupid but of whom there was scarcely any pleasing. And it certainly was much better than to have to fawn before the carping rudeness of the officials at the Unemployment Ex-change.

But as time went on it began to tell on her nerves. She fed Miss Rhona and washed her and did everything for her in the same way as she would have done things for a baby. And never once by look or by anything else did the imbecile show that she was aware of Miss Mayfield's presence. She stared straight in front of her, her black eyes dull as dead snails in her impassive yellow face as she rocked steadily backward and forward. "If she would just smile at me or look at me," Miss Mayfield wailed to Mrs. Spowart. "Gee whiz, you'd think she could surely do that. Even a baby would do something. It would look at you and laugh and hold out its arms, the little lamb, and gurgle and let you tickle it and kiss it. You'd get something in return for all you did for it. But that big fat lump . . . . . "

"Ay, it would take a gey brave yin to think about pettin' Miss Rhona," said Mrs. Spowart. "Puir thing, too."

"Puir thing nothing," said Miss Mayfield. "I could murder her sometimes, she makes me that angry. Surely to goodness she could do something for herself. It's not as if she were helpless."

For although she was misshapen Miss Rhona could walk perfectly well, and she had the full command of her limbs. She could have fed herself all right, but Miss Mayfield said it was sheer stubbornness that made her not do it. "If she'd been born like you and me, Mrs. Spowart," she said, "she'd have had to do things for herself. No wonder she's so helpless. She's been pampered. If you ask me, it's not that she can't do things, it's pure thrawnness. She's like all the rest of them who've been born with silver spoons in their mouths, she won't do a thing for herself if she can get other folk to do it for her."

Mrs. Spowart did not agree with this. She was a perfect specimen of the old family retainer, and she had been with Miss Rhona's father and mother when the imbecile was born. But Miss Mayfield had none of the cook's loyalty to the aristocratic tradition. She had had to 'fend for herself since childhood, she'd had to fight for a job and fight to keep the job, fight with the customers and fight with the boss, and now at the age of forty-seven she was still fighting to earn enough to keep her alive. Sometimes she thought she would be better dead. She had nothing to look forward to but the pension when she was sixty-five, and a lonely poverty-stricken old age, probably in the poor-house or some such institution. It seemed so senseless to slave and slave to keep herself alive with that future ahead of her.

Gradually she began to hate Miss Rhona. The loony became a symbol—a symbol of the small wealthy class who kept people like Miss Mayfield down. They sat impassively, doing nothing to help themselves, yet they got all the attention, all the luxuries.

"I could murder her," she said to the cook. "Sittin' there like a bloomin' heathen idol with her fat, smug face, lettin' me do all the dirty work for her, and never as much as a thank you. Takin' it all for granted. I wish somethin' would happen to her."

"What guid would that dae ye?" asked Mrs. Spowart. "Ye wouldnie ha'e a job then."

But Miss Mayfield thought that anything would be better than living like a slave. She would far rather go back to the drudgery of a shop, even though the wages would be smaller, than stay and wait on this creature who didn't deserve to be alive. If only something would happen to Miss Rhona!

Miss Rhona could not speak, nor could she write. But she had a way of making herself understood by just gazing fixedly at whatever she wanted. She didn't even put herself to the trouble of pointing, although she was perfectly able to do so. This infuriated Miss Mayfield. "She's lazy, that's what she is," she complained to Mrs. Spowart one night after Miss Rhona was safely in bed after a very exacting evening. "Thinks she's Lord God Almighty. Gee whiz, she couldn't be any more trouble if she was. I wonder what she'd do if we didn't take any notice of her?"

That was an idea. Miss Mayfield couldn't help thinking about it. And she thought that she would try it and see. So the next day when she was giving the loony her dinner she set a plate of soup in front of her and nodded significantly at it instead of spooning it into Miss Rhona's mouth as she usually did. She sat down to her own soup and ate it. Every now and then she glanced at the loony to see how she was getting on. But the loony sat and stared straight in front of her. Miss Mayfield finished her soup, and, knowing that Mrs. Spowart was safely out of the way, she leaned forward and poked Miss Rhona. She nodded at the soup, indicating that the loony was to take her spoon and feed herself. For a few minutes they looked at each other, Miss Mayfield's sharp green eyes glaring at the loony's sombre black ones. Then suddenly the loony acted. She lifted the plate and held it to her mouth, and then she poured the whole plateful down the front of her dress.

Miss Mayfield was furious. " I'll kill you one of these days," she hissed as she undressed the misshapen figure and put a clean dress on it. " I'll make you sorry you ever were born."

The idiot stared back at her without a flicker of understanding.

After that Miss Mayfield did everything she could to try to humiliate the loony and get her to retaliate in some way in order to have a good excuse for striking her. But all her efforts were in vain. The loony stared uncomprehendingly at her, as silent and as ugly as a gargoyle. And day after day, hating her, Miss Mayfield wondered more and more what would happen if anything happened to Miss Rhona.

It would be so easy for something to happen. She might fall down the stairs and break her neck, or she might cut herself, or . . . . . well, there were lots of ways in which she might suddenly cease living.

Miss Mayfield was terrified suddenly at the trend in which she found her thoughts moving.

She tried to dismiss them from her mind, surprised that a respectable woman like herself could have such thoughts. She wasn't the kind of person who did those kind of things. What would she gain, anyway? Nothing but the loss of a job and subsequent unemployment, as Mrs. Spowart had pointed out. Ach, don't be daft, she said to herself, you know you would never have the nerve, anyway.

Nevertheless, it was pleasant to think about it, to feel that she might be one of these women whose photographs adorned the pages of the more sensational newspapers. And almost unconsciously she found her mind dwelling more and more upon the possibility of Miss Rhona coming to a sudden end by her hand. Of course, she would never have have the courage to carry her plans into action, but it was nice to see what she could think up in the way of a perfect murder.

She tried to imagine what anybody who really intended to murder the loony would do. They would need to have a motive, of course. They would need to be after the loony's money or something. They would have to have a better motive than mere hatred. Although God knows that it was strong enough at times, so strong that it took all her time to keep her hands away from Miss Rhona's thick neck.

What would the murderer do? Which method would he apply? Strangling and poison and a knife—all these were hopeless. Nobody who wanted to throw the police off the scent would consider these. Suffocation? Well, that would be easy enough. All they needed to do was to get the loony into bed and then hold the bedclothes over her.

No, on second thoughts, that idea wasn't so good. A far better way would be gas. Miss Rhona could be enticed into the kitchen when Mrs. Spowart was out, the gas turned on, and the door locked with the loony inside.

Miss Mayfield sighed at her lack of imagination. She would not make a good murderer. Everything she thought of was so obvious that the police would spot it at once.

Nevertheless, her imagination kept dwelling on various possibilities. And it was fed by her growing hatred. Things got to such a pitch between the loony and herself that often she thought of leaving. But the remembrance of the slights her pride had received at the Unemployment Exchange stopped her. Certainly her pride boggled at the menial tasks she was forced to perform for the loony, but there was this advantage: she could get her own back on the loony in a number of petty ways, such as pinching and slapping and tormenting, all with the knowledge that the poor dumb creature couldn't tell. Sometimes Miss Mayfield was surprised to find what a cruel streak was appearing in her nature. What between thinking of new methods of torturing Miss Rhona and dwelling on the various ways in which she could be murdered, Miss Mayfield had become a completely different character.

Then one day as she was taking the loony downstairs she had an idea. It's true that she had thought of it before, but it had never quite struck her like this. It was so simple. And it was so clever and unsuspicious in its simplicity. Everybody would naturally think that the loony had stumbled.

All that day Miss Mayfield watched the loony, watched her like the proverbial spider. She gloated over what she had thought of doing. Rolling the idea round her mind, relishing it as her palate would have relished a delicacy. Towards evening it became too good to keep. She must share it with somebody.

And who better could she share it with than the intended victim? As she put the loony to bed she told her. She put her face close to the dull yellow mask, her own features twisting with pent-up hatred. "Hah!" she hissed. "I'll soon put an end to you, my bonnie wee hen. We'll see what good your money will do you tomorrow when you get the push that'll send you sliding straight down into hell. Ha, just you wait! Better enjoy your bed tonight, for this'll be the last time."

The loony stared back with her impenetrable stare, uncomprehending and vacant. Miss Mayfield was furious; she would have liked the loony to have understood and to have savoured to the full the horror of what was coming to her.

The next morning Miss Mayfield dressed Miss Rhona carefully, dressed her as though she were dressing the poor body for a wedding. Then she took her by the arm and led her along the landing. There was no fear in Miss Mayfield's heart. She was only a little surprised at her own callousness. She led Miss Rhona to the top of the stairs. She knew there was nobody in the house but Mrs. Spowart, and she was busy in the kitchen, but she looked around, just in case .....

She put her face close to Miss Rhona's, and she gripped her shoulders and snarled: "Now, then!"

She clenched her teeth tightly together. This was her great moment, the moment she had been preparing for during all these months of accumulating hatred. If only the loony could understand what was about to happen to her ....

94

" " See ! " she hissed, and she enacted in dumb show what she was about to do, watching for signs of terror and understanding.

But Miss Rhona stared vacantly in front of her, tottering on the top step. Miss Mayfield licked her dry lips. She tightened her grip on the loony's shoulders. Now . . . . .

But there was no strength in her arms. She saw the stair yawning emptily beneath her, but she could do nothing about it.

She took the loony's arm and propelled her downstairs in front of her. She realized suddenly with horror and self-pity that this would happen again and again and that she would never have the courage to take the decisive step.

6. THE GULLS

The little boy awoke as soon as it was light. He listened, but he could hear no movements in the house. The ticking of the clock made him look towards it. Twenty past five. He knew it was too early to get up. His Aunt Julia had said he would need to get up early, but he knew that if he got up as early as this she would be annoyed. And he did not want to annoy her to-day of all days. So he lay back, waiting patiently for it to be the correct time.

He could hear the first faint chirping of birds, and through the window he could see little streaks of pink shooting up the saffron sheet of sky. He wanted to get up; to let everybody know that to-day he was going for a sail up Loch Lomond with his Aunt Julia and Uncle Sandy and his cousin, Nan, and her husband. And he wondered how he could possibly fill in the time until seven o'clock, the authorised hour for rising.

He began to count the spirals of blue on the cream-grounded wallpaper, starting from the one nearest the brass knob of his bed and mounting towards the ceiling. But when he had nearly reached the top he thought that he had missed one, and he came down and started again. He had not realized that it would be so difficult; the spirals seemed to merge into each other. Shifting up and down like waves, he thought, the waves he would see when he got to Loch Lomond . . . .

"Time to get up, Georgie." His Uncle Sandy's thin tired voice came from a great distance.

The little boy blinked sleepily. "But it's not time to get up yet," he said.

"It's seven o'clock," his aunt cried from the living-room. "If you don't rise this minute, I'll come and haul the clothes off you!"

They were finishing breakfast when Nan and her husband arrived. She was a thin pale girl of twenty-five, with a peevish face. Ted was a couple of years older, a plump young man with flashing false-teeth.

"Hello, aren't you ready yet?" he cried jovially. And he slapped Georgie on the bottom as the little boy passed him. "Get a move on, son, or we won't take you with us, will we, old man?"

As he went upstairs for his raincoat, Georgie wondered why Uncle Sandy didn't complain when Ted called him "Old man." He would, if he had been his father-in-law.

When he came downstairs, his aunt and uncle were arguing.

"You'll put on your bowler," Aunt Julia said. "You're not coming with us wearing that old cap."

"But it's comfortable," Uncle Sandy said. "And I can always take it off and put it in my pocket."

"You're not coming one step with it," Aunt Julia said. "You look like a tramp!"

"Better put on your bowler, old man," Ted said. "We've all got to be dressed when we go on holiday."

"To damn with you," Uncle Sandy said, but he slowly took off his old cap and hung it up. "You want me to be dressed like a prize rabbit," he said as he brushed his bowler with his sleeve.

"And put your gloves on," Aunt Julia said, giving her hat another tilt before the mirror. "I'm sure you might have scrubbed your nails. What mourning hems! You should be ashamed of them. Put your gloves on and hide them, for any favour!"

They caught the ten-past-eight bus at the corner of the street. Ted led the way to the front. "Here's a seat, ma,"

G   97

he said, pushing Aunt Julia into an empty seat. Nan sat down beside her mother, and Uncle Sandy and Ted sat in the seat in front. Georgie had to stand. He refused to sit on Ted's knee when the young man tried to pull him onto it.

"Four twos and a half," Ted said to the conductor.

The conductor punched the tickets and held them out. "There you are, old man," Ted said, and Uncle Sandy reached into his trousers-pocket and paid.

At the Waverley Station Ted said: "I think you should just get singles to Lochearnhead; we'll come back by bus."

"But we're going to Balloch," Uncle Sandy said.

"I know you said that," Ted said. "But don't you think it would be a better plan to go to Lochearnhead? Nan and I were talking about it last night, and we thought we had seen Loch Lomond so often that it would be a good plan to go somewhere else."

"But we promised Georgie we'd go to Loch Lomond," Uncle Sandy said.

"Georgie won't mind," Ted said. "Will you, Georgie?"

"I want to go to Loch Lomond," Georgie said.

"Oh, come on now!" Ted said.

Georgie looked appealingly at Aunt Julia.

"What about it, Bo'sun?" Uncle Sandy said. •

"I think we should go to Loch Lomond," Aunt Julia said. "After all, we made up our minds to go there."

Ted shrugged sulkily and slouched onto a seat while Uncle Sandy went to the Booking-office. "I'll give you the money for our tickets after," he called after his father-in-law, but Georgie knew that he never would.

"Loch Lomond will be like hell on a day like this," Ted said. "All those infernal Glasgow trippers will be there."

"We don't need to mix with them," Aunt Julia said, sighing with pleasure as she allowed her fourteen stone to relax on the seat beside Ted. "What a time your father's taking!"

"There's a big queue at the Booking-office," Nan said.

"He doesn't need to be as slow as all that, though," Aunt Julia said. She tried to stretch her short neck to see where her husband was, panting with the exertion. "Who's this he's got into tow with now?" she exclaimed angrily.

Georgie stopped fiddling with a slot-machine and watched his uncle approach with a seedy-looking man. He heard his aunt cluck with disapproval.

"The train goes from Platform Three," Uncle Sandy cried jovially. "Meet the wife," he said to the stranger. "This is Mr. Noble. He's going to Balloch, too."

"How do you do?" Aunt Julia bowed frigidly.

Mr. Noble was a tall thin man, but his belly stuck out like a balloon. He bobbed his thin head at them, and Georgie watched with fascination as the drip at the end of his red nose splashed onto the platform.

"Where did the old man pick up that?" Ted whispered as he walked between his wife and his mother-in-law in the wake of Uncle Sandy and Mr. Noble.

"How should I know?" Aunt Julia sniffed. "Really, your father for picking up all sorts of queer people!"

They found an empty carriage. Aunt Julia and Nan and Ted sat with their backs to the engine; Uncle Sandy, Mr. Noble and Georgie opposite them. Georgie knelt on the seat and kept his face flattened to the window for most of the journey. His uncle and the stranger talked all the time. They tried to draw the three others into their conversation, but without success. Georgie wondered why Aunt Julia should be so quiet; she usually talked such a lot. And it was not like Ted to be so silent. He and Aunt Julia usually dominated the conversation. Occasionally he looked at Ted's supercilious expression and at the way Aunt Julia kept jerking her head and swallowing as though something were sticking in her throat. He began to wonder why they did not talk to Mr. Noble. If he had not been so interested in the journey and in the fact that he was going to Loch Lomond he would have been only too glad to listen to Mr. Noble and his uncle; they talked of so many interesting things. Especially Mr. Noble, who was a piano-tuner, and who had many funny stories to tell about the people whose pianos he had tuned.

But the journey overshadowed everything. The little boy wondered if he would be able to paddle at Loch Lomond. And would there be donkeys there as there were at the seaside?

As soon as they got into Queen Street Station in Glasgow, Aunt Julia seized Georgie by the arm and hurried him towards the barrier. "Don't you dare look round," she said.

She held out her own and Georgie's tickets to the collector, then she hustled the little boy through the Glasgow forenoon crowds into the Third Class Ladies' Waiting Room. "You sit here," she said, pushing him into a seat in the corner. "And don't you dare look out of that door."

Obediently he sat down on the shiny wooden seat and stared at his bare knees while his aunt disappeared. He had been sitting for about two minutes when Nan came in. She stood inside the doorway, craning her thin neck. "Where's my mother?" she asked Georgie.

He pointed to the door through which Aunt Julia had gone. Nan darted towards it, her long neck stretched out like an ostrich's. Georgie resumed his inspection of his knees. He picked moodily at a scab on his left knee-cap.

"If we stay here until train-time," Aunt Julia said to Nan as they re-joined Georgie, "that man'll have to get into the train by himself."

"My father's fair wild," Nan said.

"Well, let him be wild," Aunt Julia said. "I never saw the like of it! Him foisting that man onto us! Who wants to take up with common dirt like that?"

"You don't think that Ted and I are keen about him, do you?" Nan said. "We don't like him any more than you do."

"Really, your father's terrible," Aunt Julia said. "He takes up with every Tom, Dick and Harry. That man's probably a rogue."

"He looks it," Nan said.

"Your father's that soft," Aunt Julia said.

"They know you're in here," Nan said.

"Damn!" Aunt Julia said. "I thought I'd managed to give them the slip."

"We'll have to get rid of him at Balloch," Nan said.

Ted and Uncle Sandy and Mr. Noble were waiting at the platform where the train for Balloch was to leave. "Hurry up!" Uncle Sandy cried. "Train leaves in a minute."

He took hold of Aunt Julia by the arm. Mr. Noble took her other arm, and they hurried her along the platform. Nan and Ted pulled Georgie along between them.

"We'll have to tell that bloke where he gets off," Ted said to his wife over the little boy's head.

"How?" she said.

"I'll soon think of something," Ted said.

He pushed Georgie into the compartment, knocking him roughly against Mr. Noble. He did not trouble to apologise. He sat down between his wife and his mother-in-law and he stared gloomily at the picture of a L.M.S. hotel above his father-in-law's head for most of the journey.

Georgie listened to his uncle and Mr. Noble, wondering why his aunt and cousins didn't like the stranger. He did not look like a rogue at all. He was a very nice man. A much nicer man, Georgie thought, than Ted. He had never been fond of Ted, but he liked him less than ever to-day. He looked at Ted's mouth, wondering why he had never noticed before that Ted's false-teeth were too big for him. Mr. Noble didn't have false-teeth. His teeth weren't very good, but they were clean. Ted's teeth were always sort of yellowish.

It was very sunny when they came out of Balloch Station.

"Well, we'll have to say good-bye here," Aunt Julia said brightly, putting out her hand to Mr. Noble. "We're going to have lunch with relations."

"It's been very pleasant meeting you," Mr. Noble said, shaking hands. "The journey passed very pleasantly."

"Yes, didn't it?" Aunt Julia said.

"But——" Uncle Sandy said.

"Come along, dear," Aunt Julia cried, taking him by the arm. "We'll have to hurry. We promised Dorothy we'd be there by one o'clock."

"Good-bye." Ted grinned flashily as he shook hands with Mr. Noble. "Good-bye."

"Good-bye." Mr. Noble smiled in a lost sort of way and turned. "Good-bye," he said again, turning round after a few steps.

"Good-bye," Aunt Julia called.

Uncle Sandy was standing with a stupid expression on his face. His wife shook his arm. "Come on, don't stand there like a stooky," she cried.

"But we've no relations in Balloch," Uncle Sandy said. "Who's this Dorothy when she's at home?"

"Who do you think she is?" Aunt Julia laughed angrily. "I made her up, of course, you old fool. Do you think we wanted to be saddled with that awful-like cratur' all day?"

"He's a very nice man," Uncle Sandy said, unwillingly matching his steps to theirs.

"You're the only one who thinks so," Ted said.

"A piano-tuner!" Aunt Julia said. "The chorus is believe it if you like! He looks a proper rogue. I'm surprised at you, Sandy Willis, taking up with a common cratur' like that."

Uncle Sandy said nothing, and he remained silent until they stopped before a very expensive-looking hotel.

"This looks the very dab," Ted said, looking up at the huge sign and the garish decorations on the front of the building.

"It doesn't look the sort of place—" Uncle Sandy began dubiously.

But before he could say any more, his wife and the two younger people began to climb the steps. Uncle Sandy looked at Georgie and sighed. "Come on, laddie, I suppose we'll just have to follow suit."

Georgie felt that his uncle was very uncomfortable and annoyed as they followed a waiter into the dining-room crowded with fashionably-dressed people. The little boy was too young and unselfconscious to feel embarrassed, but something told him that the stout middle-aged man felt out of place.

Aunt Julia and Nan and Ted followed the waiter with confident steps, however. Aunt Julia sailed in front, her head cocked a little to the side, the ornament in her blue straw hat sticking up jauntily.

The waiter led them to a table in the corner of the room. He was pulling out a chair for her when Aunt Julia stopped him.

"Is that table over there engaged?" she asked loudly in what she thought was an ultra-genteel accent.

" No, madam."

" We'll sit there then." And she led the way to a table in the centre of the dining-room.

" What did you want to sit here for?" Uncle Sandy whispered hoarsely when the waiter had gone with their order.

" What do you think?" Aunt Julia whispered back. " To see and be seen, of course." She sat up straight and jerked her shoulders. With a half-smile that gave her a sarcastic look, she turned this way and that, eyeing the other diners.

Georgie was sitting opposite Ted, who had his chest thrown out and who was looking around aggressively.

" Very crowded here to-day, isn't it?" Ted said.

Uncle Sandy mumbled something.

" Yes, it's terribly crowded," Aunt Julia said.

She put her elbows on the table and clasped her hands, smiling over them at Ted.

Uncle Sandy winked at Georgie. " Your auntie's a dab at doin' the laddiedah, isn't she?"

Georgie grinned.

" Take your hands off the table, George," said Aunt Julia. " How often have I to learn you manners?"

" Oh to damn, can you not leave the bairn alone?" Uncle Sandy said. " He's on holiday."

Aunt Julia glared at him, and he looked down at his plate. He looked at his plate during most of the lunch, looking up only occasionally to grin or wink at Georgie when Aunt Julia or Ted said something fatuous. He ate his food hurriedly, shovelling it into his mouth in noisy gulps. Aunt Julia picked at her meat with finicky gestures, and from time to time watched the people at the other tables. Ted kept his chest puffed out and looked around with a self-satisfied air while he chewed. Nan scarcely ever looked up from the table. Unconsciously she drew her thin body towards the shelter of her father. Georgie was the only one who behaved exactly as he would have behaved at home.

He saw his uncle sigh with relief when he had spooned the last fragment of meringue into his mouth. " Well, that's that," Uncle Sandy said, wiping his mouth with his handkerchief. " Are you all ready for the road?"

"We'll have coffee," Aunt Julia said, signalling the waiter.

"Oh to damn, woman, what do you want to bother with that for?"

"Will you bring coffee, please?" Aunt Julia ordered the waiter.

Uncle Sandy shook his head at Georgie. "Do you want to be bothered wi' thae sniffellin' wee cups?" he said.

Georgie grinned sympathetically. He gripped the small cup with two fingers, as he saw the others do, but he made a face when he tasted the black coffee. He took only a few sips.

"Bring my bill, please," Ted said in a lordly way to the waiter when they had finished.

Disdainfully he picked the folded bill from the tray and laid it on the table. "Thank you," he said coldly. He took his case from his waistcoat-pocket, opened it with a flourish and offered his cigarettes to his father-in-law.

As he held out a match for Uncle Sandy, he glanced around to see that nobody was looking, then he pushed the bill across the table.

"That's the bill, paw," he said.

It was the first time that Georgie had heard him speak in a low voice since they entered the dining-room.

"Let me see it," Aunt Julia said, and she picked it up and scrutinised it. She pushed it over to Uncle Sandy. Then furtively she picked up a slice of cake and pushed it into Georgie's pocket, saying: "They've charged us for it."

They wandered around Balloch for a while, then they went down to the pier for the two o'clock boat. There were few passengers aboard *The Fair Maid Of Perth* yet. Uncle Sandy and Ted went up on deck to get a good view of the town. Georgie wanted to go with them, but his aunt dragged him down into the saloon with herself and Nan.

They did not come up until after the boat had started. Georgie was hanging behind to look at the engines, but his aunt called impatiently for him to hurry up. "You'll dirty your suit," she said. "Look at your hands already. They're filthy."

" My goodness!" she exclaimed angrily as they came on deck. " Here's that man again!"

Georgie noticed that Uncle Sandy was looking brighter than he had been since they said good-bye to Mr. Noble before lunch. As for the piano-tuner himself, he was looking very gay. He raised his bowler hat with a flourish when he saw Aunt Julia.

" I'm glad to have run up against you again, Mrs. Willis," he said.

Aunt Julia bowed frigidly.

" Did you have a nice time with your friends?" Mr. Noble said.

" Very nice," Aunt Julia said. " Thank you."

She and Nan and Ted sat on a seat and stared at the water and the hills as the boat glided up the loch. They said nothing until Uncle Sandy and Mr. Noble went down to the bar in the saloon, then Aunt Julia began a long harangue about Mr. Noble. Georgie was leaning on the rail, feeling very tired. He was disappointed that there were no donkeys. He tried to make up for their absence by watching the seagulls skimming over the waves, and he listened half-heartedly to what his aunt was saying.

" .....just a common vulgar social climber," Aunt Julia said. " Fastening himself onto us like that ....."

" Whisht, mother," Nan said. " Here they come."

Uncle Sandy and Mr. Noble were laughing heartily as they swaggered along the deck. They had cigars stuck in their mouths. Mr. Noble was carrying a big box of chocolates. He stopped before Aunt Julia and presented it with a flourish.

" Oh, I couldn't!" Aunt Julia cried. " I'm fair ashamed to take it."

But Mr. Noble made a lordly gesture and moved on with Uncle Sandy. Georgie looked from his aunt's red face to the backs of the two swaggering men. Two or three seagulls were fluttering over the deck. One of them swooped close to where Uncle Sandy, his head thrown back, was strutting with Mr. Noble. And as Georgie watched, a splash of white fell on top of his uncle's bowler

Georgie looked at his aunt and cousins, but none of them had noticed. Ted and Nan were watching Aunt Julia with greedy eyes as her plump fingers opened the box of chocolates.

The little boy began to laugh. He felt very tired and disappointed, but he hung onto the rail and laughed wildly, not very sure what he was laughing at. His aunt and cousins stared enquiringly at him.

"The gulls!" he spluttered. "Aren't the gulls funny?"

7. THE MATINEE

All forenoon he had swaggered so proudly in his new trousers that his mother was astonished when he changed into shorts at dinner-time.

"What's wrang wi' yer longs?" she said. "Are ye feared folk'll laugh at ye?"

"No," Henry said. "I'm goin' to the matinee at the Palace."

"But ye can gang in yer longs."

"I want to get in for a half," Henry said.

"Ye've got a hope!" his mother said. "Ye're past four-teen an' ye're big for yer age."

"I'll try, onyway," Henry said. "They're givin' prizes the day. Ye get a number wi' yer ticket an' if they draw yer number ye get a prize."

"A surprise!" his mother said, accentuating the pun. "That's what ye'll get. Dinnie expect me to come an' bail ye oot if they arrest ye for fraud!"

Henry laughed boastfully. "No bloomin' fear!"

He took his little brother, Ian, with him. Ian was seven. It wasn't his company that Henry wanted, although it gave him a sense of superiority to swagger along manfully with Ian running to keep up with him. He hoped to win a prize. If he did, he would send Ian up to the platform to get it for him. He thought of everything, did Henry! There were no flies on him!

All the same, his knees felt cold. He wished that he had kept on his longs. Still—sixpence admission wearing them was more than outbalanced by twopence admission without them! Fourpence in his pocket was much more satisfying meantime that the self-conscious glow of manhood's estate. You couldn't have it both ways! So to console himself for any fancied diminishment of his glory, he bought a packet of Woodbines before he and Ian reached the Palace.

His knees sagged as he approached the pay-box.

"Two halves, please," he said.

His voice was breaking, and he had difficulty in making it as childish as he would have wished. But the girl apparently noticed nothing unusual in the strange quaver; she swept up the four pennies and handed him two tickets. He was turning away with a sense of something accomplished, when the girl cried:

"Here! Wait a minute."

His bowels contracted with fear, and his knees felt colder than ever. Their bare boniness seemed a long way down. He tried to squeeze his head and shoulders nearer to them as he returned nervously to the little bowl.

"You've forgotten your lucky numbers," the girl said, handing him two slips of paper.

He took them with relief and hurried Ian across the entrance-hall, down a corridor to the door marked "Stalls." He clutched Ian firmly by the arm, wishing that the difference in their heights was not so obvious.

He handed the tickets to the girl at the door. She took them in an absent-minded way and tore them across. She was languidly handing him back half of them when she seemed suddenly to jump to life.

"How old are you?" she said suspiciously.

"E—eleven," he said in a small, frightened voice.

"And how!" the girl said. "You're surely a Glaxo baby! Are there many more at home like you?"

She waved them on and nonchalantly returned to the contemplation of her finger nails. Henry hastily pushed Ian into an empty row of seats and sat down before anybody else could comment on his size. He tried to shrivel up into as small bulk as possible. That had been a near thing!

The picture house was as dim as a temple. The lamps, hanging like obscure oranges out of the murkiness of the roof, intensified the apostolic atmosphere. The place was about half-full of children, all congregated in the seats nearest the screen. They made a frightful noise as they waited for the performance to begin, like imps chanting an incantation before the vast white altar of the screen. They *were* imps. They worshipped the Movie mammon, they prayed to the cinema-god to give them drugs to help them forget their belly-hunger and their poorly-clad bodies. They gazed intently at the blank screen, while they waited for it to answer their worshipping prayers and their devoted weekly pilgrimages with their twopences to its shrine. This was their god. This was their temple. And this was their prayer.

One, two, three, four, five, six, seven, eight, nine, ten!
For they thought that the performance would begin as soon as they had shouted *ten*. But they were wrong. The screen remained overpoweringly blank. So they began hopefully to count again, drawing out the space between *nine* and *ten* into a huge bubble of expectancy and shouting *ten* at the pitch of their voices. But the bubble was shattered. Nothing happened.

Henry sat with a tolerant smile on his face. He had re-covered from his fright. He felt very old and experienced beside these kids. And he dug Ian with his elbow when the little boy added his shrill treble to the din.

"Don't!" he hissed angrily.

Henry's seat was at the end of a row, so he crossed his legs and stuck them out into the aisle. He felt very manly and superior as he took out his packet and lit a Woodbine. He had forgotten his fear of the attendant. If only he had on his longs he would have been perfectly happy!

But then, none of the kids would have been able to see them in this dim light. He was better with his fourpence.

The first picture was a cowboy film. You saw them only at kids' matinees nowadays. Henry felt very grown up and sophisticated as he leaned back to watch it. He tried to appear bored by the hair-raising escapades of the hero, and he angrily checked Ian when the little boy gave vent to his feelings.

Ian, however, was not alone in his excitement. All the children were yelling hysterical encouragement to "the goodie" in his efforts to outwit the evil schemes of "the baddie." They made so much noise that Henry could not hear a word that was being said on the screen. He started to feel annoyed, but he checked himself when he remembered that he wasn't interested in the picture, anyway. Ian was jumping up and down in his seat, and when the villain, with a knife in his hand, crept up behind the hero, he stood and shrieked with the others:

"Shot, mister! Here's the baddie!"

Henry was disgusted. He lighted another Woodbine. He twisted his face into what he fondly hoped was a sardonic smile and thought: What kids! And he puffed nonchalantly while the hero galloped on the back of his trusty steed to free the heroine from the mine in which the villain had imprisoned her. There were close-ups of her every minute or two between shots of the hero and his horse and close-ups of the fuse the villain had lighted to blow up the mine. The children were frantic with excitement. "Go on! Go on!" they screamed hoarsely to the galloping cowboy. And "She's in there mister!" when the hero finally arrived at the mine and did not know in which tunnel to look for her.

Henry tried to make the smoke come down his nose, but his attempt failed dismally. He coughed and spluttered. And the tears ran down his cheeks. He hoped nobody would notice and think that he was crying because the hero looked as if he wasn't going to find the heroine in time.

Henry knew he would. The hero always arrived in time. Then there was a clinch. His interest was momentarily aroused here, but before the hero could do more than take the girl in his arms, there was a fade-out and *The End* was flashed on the screen.

"Gee, Henry, wasn't it great?" Ian said.

"Suits kids," Henry said in a lordly manner.

The principal picture was "The Loyal Worker," featuring Granby Dexter and Vera Varden. Henry liked Granby Dexter. He had seen him in six pictures already. In this one he worked in a mill and he was in love with the boss's daughter. Right at the beginning of the picture you got a close-up of him watching the girl—it was Vera Varden and she was pretty hot—through the window of his workshop. The picture was taken from behind Granby Dexter so that you could get a good look at his wavy hair and his straight nose.

"Is he the goodie, Henry?" Ian said.

"Shuttup and lookit the picter," Henry said, never taking his eyes off the screen.

"I'm gonna marry that dame," Granby Dexter said.

"Swell chance you got," a workman said.

Just then Vera Varden dropped her handkerchief without noticing it, and Granby Dexter left his machine and ran and got it for her. He shouldn't have left his machine, but his workmate attended to it till he came back after he'd stood a while speaking to Vera Varden. The next scene was a dinner party at the boss's house and Granby was there. He looked great. Much better than the rich man who thought he was going to get Vera Varden.

After that you saw the mill-hands talking among themselves and complaining about their poor pays. And one of them said: "They can't keep us down for ever. They'll press us and press us, but one of these days they'll press too hard and we'll spring back at them. They'll have only themselves to blame." So they decided to go on strike. But Granby Dexter wouldn't go on strike. No, sir, he would remain true to the boss and the boss's daughter. "You're fools," he said to the strikers. "The boss is your best friend." And when they attacked him he socked about a dozen of them before the police arrived and socked some more. Then he stood at the gates of the mill and said that he at least would remain loyal, that he'd keep the flag flying. And Vera Varden laid her hand on his sleeve and said: "Gee, big boy, you're wonderful!"

Oh, it was romantic. Henry's mouth was half open. He wished vaguely that Ian would stop wriggling so much, but he couldn't take his attention off the screen for a moment to check him.

"Henry," Ian said.

"Aw, shuttup and lookit the picter," Henry said.

Henry lighted another Woodbine and puffed it furiously while Granby Dexter made love to Vera Varden. He wished that his hair would wave like Granby's instead of sticking up on the crown so that no amount of water would make it lie down.

The strikers' wives and children were starving, so Granby and Vera went to their homes with food. The wives were so pleased that they kissed Vera Varden's hand and stroked the sleeves of her fur coat. Their men stood in the background and glowered. All the same, they looked pretty sorry for themselves. They sniffed and they had tears in their eyes.

" Henry," Ian said persistently.

" What is it?"

Ian whispered something.

" Well, go on," Henry said.

" But I don't know where the place is."

" Well, I'm not taking you," Henry said. " You'll need to wait till the picter's finished."

The strikers were getting desperate. They came to the gates of the mill and appealed to Vera Varden's father. He said he'd take them back on the old terms. " You aren't the only ones who're suffering, boys," he said. " I gotta child, too." Granby Dexter stood beside the boss with a revolver in each hand in case the strikers got nasty. " You should be loyal like this brave fellow," the boss said.

Henry wished he worked for a boss who had a daughter he could marry. He wouldn't join any strike. No, sir! He would be loyal like Granby Dexter.

" Henry, I'm awful needin'," Ian whimpered.

" You'll have to wait," Henry snarled.

His eyes were sticking out of his head. He was so interested that he forgot to puff his cigarette. And he leaned forward eagerly, wondering if the starving women would prevail upon their husbands to return to work. See, one of them was lifting a little child up to its grim, iron-jawed father.

" Daddy, I'm hungry," the child lisped.

Henry sniffed sympathetically when the father drew his sleeve across his eyes and turned away.

"Do what the boss tells you," the woman said. "He's a good boss."

"You said it, sister!" another woman said. "Might is always right."

So the strikers went back meekly to the mill, and as they filed past the boss they took off their hats humbly. He stood with his belly thrust out and he placidly shifted his cigar from one corner of his mouth to the other. Granby Dexter and Vera Varden were hugging each other beside him.

The last scene, showing their wedding-carriage being drawn through the streets by the happy-to-be-back-at-work men, was spoiled for Henry by the persistent entreaties of Ian and by his agitated wriggling.

"I'm bustin'," he snivelled.

"All right," Henry said gruffly. "Just a minute."

But it was more than a minute before the romantic close-up between Vera and Granby had faded out, and allowed Henry to rise and haul Ian up the aisle after him.

Henry stopped at the door and looked back. None of the other children were following them, although the lights had gone up. Was there to be another picture? Henry hesitated. Ian tugged impatiently at him.

A man came on the platform in front of the screen and said: "We'll now draw to-day's lucky numbers. Will some little boy or girl come up here and draw the numbers?"

"C'mon, Henry," Ian entreated.

But Henry didn't move. He watched a little girl mince sedately on the platform and wave coyly to her friends in the audience while waiting for the bag with the numbers to be handed to her. He gripped Ian savagely by the shoulder. "Stand still," he said.

He listened intently as the man read out the numbers the girl drew from the bag.

"Two-hundred-and-four."

There was a moment's silence while everybody looked round inquiringly for the lucky holder of the number. At last a stout boy perspiringly mounted the steps and received a teddy-bear.

There was much noisy laughter and a few cat-calls. The manager waited for silence before he read out the next

numbers. "One-hundred-and-thirty-six.... One-hundred-
and-eighty...."

Henry had one-hundred-and-eighty.

"Here, Ian," he said. "You go for the prize."

Ian made no move. He gazed up piteously at Henry's
face.

"Go on," Henry said.

"I can't," Ian wailed.

* * *

"Well, *I* couldn't help it, could I?" Henry said later,
trying to explain to his mother. "It wasn't me that made
him do it."

8. THE BIG APPLE

"I could be cute," the fat girl at the next table said. "But, jees,.what's the use?" she said.

"That's right, honey," the other girl said. "What's the use?"

They stared disconsolately at the table for a while, then when they'd finished their drinks they called for more.

Louis and Mac came in and sat down at my table. They looked tired and disgusted and hungry. They said nothing.

"What's on your minds?" I said.

Mac put a couple of rejection-slips on the table and Louis put four rejection-slips on the table. They stared at them as if they were gamblers putting their shirts on a game of poker. I put down a couple of rejection-slips and a cheque. It was for seven-and-sixpence. They both grabbed it.

"Hell, is that all?" Mac said.

"What more do you expect for a review?" I said.

"I thought that maybe *Life and Letters To-Day* had bought a poem or you'd sold a story to *The Fortnightly*," Louis said.

"You'd better think again," I said.

I ordered three beers. We sipped them for a while. Then Louis said: "What was the review?"

"*Gone With The Grape-Fruit,*" I said.

"That book," Mac said.

"Well," I said, "I wouldn't have got it if I hadn't been in America for a year."

We all finished our beer. The fat girl was drawing her powder-puff listlessly down her cheeks. I ordered another three beers.

"Anyway, it's selling well," I said. "It's sold about a quarter of a million copies already."

"Yes, but what a book!" Louis said.

"Maybe we should try to write something like that," I said. "Maybe we would get somewhere writing a book like that instead of writing stuff nobody 'll take."

"Maybe we should sweep the streets," Mac said.

"Maybe we do," I said. "The last editor I showed that dock-yard story to said as much."

"What's wrong with us, anyway?" Louis said.

"What's wrong with everybody?" I said.

I looked around. The place was full of old buns and pansies. There were maybe a hundred people in that cafe and most of them were cockeyed. And it was only one cafe in London. And London is only one city in the whole of the British Empire. And the British Empire is only one part of the world.

"Maybe we should try to write something like *Gone With The Grape-Fruit,*" I said. "Something sweet and clean and wholesome."

"Don't make me laugh," Mac said.

"No, but you'd laugh all right if you were getting the sales," I said.

Louis said maybe we'd better collaborate on a book like that. If the three of us wrote it it wouldn't take so long and we could write it under a nom-de-plume so that we wouldn't feel so bad about it. Mac said that was all very well but what were we going to write about.

"About life," I said.

"But we write about life already," he said. "That's the reason why nobody will take the stuff we write."

I guess he was right. We write about life all right: life in the raw, but it's so raw that nobody can stomach it.

What we should write about is something sweet and sickly, something that will make people forget that there are such things as prostitution and kids going hungry and men working long hours for small pays and graft and disease and rich men getting richer off the arms-racket, the blood of the soldiers and the sweat of the workers. What people want to read about is the life they think they should lead. They want to think they are so much better than they are.

" What'll we take for a pen-name? " Louis said.

" Something sloppy," I said.

" A woman's name," Mac said. " Look at all the women who've written that sort of stuff."

" Minnie something," I said.

" Minnie the Moocher," Louis said.

" Bessie or Clara or Jane," Mac said.

" Nancy," Louis said. " Nancy B. Nice."

" Don't be personal," Mac said.

" Kitty," I said, looking at the fat girl. " Kitty B. Kute."

" What about a title? " Louis said.

We ordered three more beers and while we were waiting for them we thought about a title. But none of the titles we thought of were any good until Mac said: " *The Years Between.*"

" The years between what? " I said.

" It looks as if it's the years between drinks," Louis said. But just then the waiter came with our beers and we grabbed them and felt more like thinking up a difficult thing like a title.

" We'll take the old gag," Mac said. " Boy meets girl. We'll make them meet in a car-crash, something exciting."

" Better make it topical," Louis said. " An aeroplane crash."

" Ay, that'll do," Mac said. " The hero is an aviator and he crashes and the girl helps him and it's a case of love at first sight. But the girl has a scheming step-mother who wants her to marry the villain and she pours oil onto love's young dream and they get separated. And that's what makes the years between. Boy, it'll knock 'em dead."

" If it doesn't knock us dead first," I said.

But Louis objected to this. He said *The Years Between* wasn't a snappy enough title. What we wanted was something topical, something that was in everybody's mouths.

" The Big Apple," Mac said.

And so there we were in this cafe in London, three young writers who were going to write a best-seller that was going to knock people dead, sitting in this cafe called The Big Apple that was full of old buns and pansies who were all cockeyed. And I guess we were a bit cockeyed ourselves though we had no illusions that maybe we would win the Nobel Prize for Literature. All we thought was maybe we would make enough money to go to New York or Prague or Egypt or the Taj Mahal or the Hanging Gardens of Babylon. Provided, that was, that all those places were left after the war was over. All we wanted was to go tarpon-fishing or to go with a caravan through Darkest Africa or to go to Tibet and visit the High Llama. Of course, as Mac, being Scotch and trying to be cynical, pointed out, the Nobel Prize for Literature was a lot of money. But we couldn't hope to get it until we were old men of about sixty with bladder-trouble and the dry rot pretty well all through our systems. We would look kind of goofy riding on camels through the sands of the desert when we were like that. We wanted the money now while we were young. And so to hell with the Nobel Prize for Literature, I said.

" That goes for me, too," Louis said.

And so we decided that although we couldn't hope to win the Nobel Prize for Literature we would write a book for the big clean British public and the big clean American public (because I am keen on the American public because they have something we haven't got. Peace, anyway, of a kind.) And it would be a book for the big clean German public and the big clean Italian public, maybe even for the big clean Japanese public if we were all through fighting by that time and had time to read a book. And it would be a book that would be in every clean fine-spirited British home on top of the piano beside the *Bible* and *East Lynne* and *Gone With the Grape-Fruit*. We decided all this sitting there in this cafe in London that is called The Big Apple and which is exactly the same as fifty other cafes in London and exactly the same as fifty other cafes in every city in the world, some of them just newly called The Big Apple because you've got to move with the times and be up-to-date and some of them called The Ritz or The Sunflower or what have you.

And once we had decided to write the book we ordered more drinks and we sat back drinking them and looking around because every text-book of writing tells us young writers that what we should write about is life and especially the life that we know best. And so we sat around in this dug-out called The Big Apple that we were all habituees of and we sipped our drinks and studied life.

"I could be cute," the fat girl was saying to the table because her girl-friend had passed out. "But I'd need to go on a diet, and hell what's the use?"

A quadroon in a white dress was singing in the middle of the dance floor, but you could hardly hear her for the noise the people at the tables were making. There was a lot of sailors and two of them were sitting with their arms around each other's necks singing *M is for Mother*. Another one was under a table with his arms tight around a girl's legs, but she was so busy drinking she didn't notice anything. Pretty nearly everybody was cockeyed or if they weren't cockeyed they were doing their best to get that way as quickly as possible. As soon as the coloured girl stopped singing they all applauded, stamping and clapping their hands as if they were crazy although they couldn't have heard one word the girl was singing. And then everybody got up to dance The Big Apple.

The Big Apple. . . . The Big Apple. . . . They swayed and they shook and they shimmied. They kicked out their legs and they wriggled their bottoms. Everybody was crazy about the Big Apple. There were white faces and red faces, even yellow faces; faces shiny with sweat and faces doped with drink; sullen faces and smiling faces; faces that grinned like the masks of long-dead mummies; all on top of legs that were doing the Big Apple. The saxophones moaned about the Big Apple. The quadroon stood in front of the band and sang into a microphone about the Big Apple. Those who were sitting at the tables watched the Big Apple. Everybody was doing the Big Apple. They were doing the Big Apple in fifty other night-clubs in London, and they were doing the Big Apple in fifty other night-clubs in every city in the world. All over the world they were doing the Big Apple.

And I sat drinking my beer and wondered how I could slip something about the world being like a big apple, a big shiny apple that looked good but which was full of maggots, into this book we were going to write. And while I was thinking this I watched the two sailors still with their arms around each other's necks get up and begin to do the Big Apple. They were so cockeyed they bumped into everybody, but they didn't mind and they looked so tough and were so tight that nobody else minded either.

Mac said wasn't I going to dance, but I said no, what was the use? It looked easy, but it wasn't as easy as it looked, and anyway I'm not such a hot dancer. I said what we wanted to think about was a snappy opening for our book that was going to knock people dead. And so we ordered more drinks and sipped them and tried to figure out a snappy opening.

And one of the sailors was being sick right in the middle of the dance floor. And while I was watching for him and his pal to get bounced I thought, This is the big clean British public for which I'm going to collaborate with Louis and Mac in writing a good clean story. This is the big clean British public who editors say won't read the stories and poems I like to write, the stories and poems which will help me to get the Nobel Prize for Literature maybe when I'm an old man of about sixty with the dry rot pretty well all through my system.

And Louis must have been thinking the same as me, for he said: " How long will it take us to write this book?"

" How long did it take you to write your last novel?" I said.

" A year," he said.

" I wrote my last book in eighteen months," Mac said.

" And I wrote mine in a year plus three dozen hangovers and six weeks dodging the landlord for back-rent," I said.

And so we all had another drink. I got back sixpence change. That was all I had left out of the seven and six I'd got for giving a good review to *Gone With The Grape-Fruit* so that the big clean public like those people who were doing the Big Apple could buy it in their millions and put it on top of the piano beside the *Bible* and *East Lynne*.

"Maybe we could write this one in three months if we all laid-off what we're writing just now," I said.

But Louis wanted to write a novel about a brothel, full of character-studies of girls who'd become what they were because they had to keep an invalid mother or because they were paying a kid brother through the university or because they couldn't earn enough working in a shop or in a pants-pressing factory. And Mac wanted to write a novel about a Scotsman who said good-bye to his Highland Hills and came to London searching for fame and fortune—especially fame, because Mac, although Scotch, is young and idealistic. And I wanted to write a novel about a hobo who went all through the States looking for work and all he got was the bum's rush and fallen arches.

"It would take us three months to write this book by Kitty B. Kute," Louis said.

"Uhuh," I said.

"Anything might happen before we got it finished," Louis said.

"Uhuh," I said.

"We might all get killed in the war," Mac said.

"What are we going to do about it?" Louis said.

"What can we do about it?" I said.

"Let's have another drink," Mac said.

But I had only sixpence left and that wasn't enough. And so we sat and looked at it and we all said What was the use? And at the next table the fat girl was hanging onto the chucker-out and telling him with tears streaming down her face that she could be cute if only she went on a diet and gave up the booze. "But, jees, what's the use?" she said.

And so we rose and went out and we held onto each other as we went across the floor and we staggered into quite a lot of those who were doing the Big Apple. But nobody said anything, because what was the use? We were just another three young drunks who'd been planning to write a book which wouldn't win the Nobel Prize for Literature but which would knock the big clean British public dead.

And when we got outside and saw the electric sign THE BIG APPLE we all stood and looked at it and then we made a dash for a lavatory down a side-street. And I thought as I was sick that the big apple was rotten to the core. And I'd got a big bite out of the apple and it tasted like sawdust, and I vowed I'd never take another bite. But I know that tomorrow night Louis and Mac and I will be back in that cafe called The Big Apple planning to write this book which will never be written. And I know that the fat girl will be sitting at one of the tables with a big steak in front of her. And I know that she will say several times in the evening: "I could be cute if I went on a diet, but, jees, what's the use?"

9. NO EXPERIENCE

There was a young man who was looking for work. He was quite an ordinary young man, and it was quite an ordinary state to be in. It didn't matter what he tried or what kind of job he applied for, he couldn't get a job at all. He was a nice writer, but nobody would engage him as a clerk because he had no experience. He was charming and polite, but nobody would engage him as a shop-assistant because he had no experience. He was big and strong and husky, but no foreman would engage him as a labourer because he had no experience. And the more experience he got in hunting for jobs, the fewer jobs there were to get. He became absolutely broken-hearted, and day by day he got thinner and thinner. Everywhere he applied he was asked the same question: "Any experience?" And not even the experience of continual refusals could make him say: "Yes."

Things went on like this for a long time, then the young man died. It appeared to be the only thing that he could do without previous experience!

He died and began to float upwards. His body was so empty that it floated upwards very easily. And as he soared through the clouds the young man began to smile hopefully, thinking that soon all his troubles would be over. And he hoped that he would reach Heaven before supper-time. "I'd love to have a good feed of corned-beef and cabbage," he murmured to a passing star. It never struck him that he had only read about that delicacy; he had had no experience of tasting it.

Presently he arrived at the Pearly Gates. Everything was very quiet and peaceful. He hoped that there would be enough supper left for him, for it was very late. But surely they would know of his arrival and keep something in the oven for him—if they had ovens in Heaven!

He straightened his tie and rang the bell. And he smiled when he thought of the number of times he had straightened his tie before applying for jobs on Earth. Well, all that was finished with now! A delicious smell of steak and onions was being wafted towards him. He sniffed appreciatively. If there was anything he thought he would like better than corned-beef and cabbage, it was steak and onions. He wished they would hurry up and open the door. He rang the bell again. But still there was no answer. "Goodness," he thought, "what bad service! They need wakening up around here!" And he began to hammer at the door.

By and by he heard the sound of feet slip-slopping towards him, then the door opened and an old man with a long white beard peered out and said querulously: "What are you making all the noise about?"

"I beg your pardon," the young man said. "But I rang the bell, and I couldn't get an answer."

"No wonder," Saint Peter said. "That bell's been broken since the Battle of the Somme. There were so many people ringing at it then that it went quite out of order. What do you want, anyway?" he said.

The young man was rather taken aback. "I've come," he said. "I'm—er—I'm dead."

"So am I," said Saint Peter.

He glared impatiently at the young man. "Hurry up," he said. "I can't stand here all night. My supper'll get cold."

The young man swallowed at the mention of supper. "I want to come in," he said. "I'm dead and I've nowhere to go."

"There are a lot of people like you," Saint Peter said. "However, what are your credentials?"

"Credentials?" the young man stammered. "I didn't think you needed any."

"What nonsense!" Saint Peter snapped. "You know perfectly well that you need credentials wherever you go."

He fumbled in his robe and brought out a dirty little book, which he opened and peered at short-sightedly. "What's your name?" he said.

The young man told him.

"Age?"

"Twenty-eight."

"Married or single?"

"Single," the poor perplexed young man bleated.

"That's all to the good," the Saint said, shutting the book. "You'll have no encumbrances?"

"No, sir. Nobody but an aunt, and she's got elephantiasis."

"Can you sing?" the Saint said suddenly.

The young man was very taken aback. "I—I don't know."

Saint Peter shook his head with disgust. "Well, you should know. I wish some of you people would find out these things before you come up here. It would save so much valuable time."

He took a tuning-fork from his robe and struck it on one of the golden pillars. "Try that," he said as the echo of the tuning-fork sounded up the Milky Way.

Timidly the young man did as he was bid. And he startled even himself by the faintness of the sound that came from his throat.

"Terrible!" Saint Peter said. "We can't use you. The Choir's overflowing with altos already. There was a dreadful influx after Hitler's 1934 Purge. Have you any experience as a baritone or as a tenor?"

"No experience," the young man said, and he looked pleadingly at the Saint. "Maybe I could do better if I had something to eat? I can't sing on an empty stomach."

"That's your look-out," the Saint said. "Can you play any musical instrument?"

The young man shook his head sadly. Then he brightened up suddenly. " Oh yes, I can play with a comb and a piece of paper."

Saint Peter frowned and said wearily: " I don't need to consult the book for that. There are exactly three billion, nine million, four hundred thousand and six people with these qualifications in Heaven already. I'm sorry, I'm afraid you'll have to try elsewhere." And he began to shut the door.

" But what am I to do?" the bewildered young man cried. " Are there no jobs in Heaven at all?"

" The only job going a-begging is the job to gild the angels' wings, and you'd be no good at that; you've had no experience. You'd better try down below. There may be some vacancies in the Basement."

Saint Peter banged the door in the young man's face, then he opened it again and said: " You can say, if you like, that I sent you. It won't do any good, of course. Good night!"

Disconsolately, the young man set off down the stairs for Hell. He wished there was a lift, for he found it very hard going. His body was so light that it would persist in going upwards. Eventually, however, he managed to reach and cross the River Styx. The three-headed dog at the gates of Hell scarcely glanced at him; he was so thin that no self-respecting dog would have thought of taking a bite out of him. Besides, Cerebus was so used to feeding on bloated profiteers and fat politicians that he would not have deigned to make a meal of a thin unemployed young man.

Old Nick himself answered the young man's timid knock and cried: " Well, what do you want here?"

" Please," the young man said. " Have you any vacancies?"

" Vacancies?" Nick roared. " Are you trying to be funny? What kind of vacancies?"

" Any kind," the young man said.

" Hm." Nick scratched his chin with the fork of his tail. " Can you stoke?"

The young man thought of the supper he had just missed in Heaven. " I could if I got the chance," he said.

" You could if you got the chance!" Nick sneered. " That's what they all say. But that's no good to me. What I want to know is: Have you any experience in stoking?"

"I'm sorry," the young man said. "But I'm willing to learn."

"That's no use. We haven't time to waste with beginners. Only trained men employed. Preferably non-Union men."

"Have you nothing else?" the young man asked timidly.

"Can you pull a barrow?"

Hope sprung up in the young man's breast. "I—I think so."

"Thinking's no good," Nick said. "What we want here are references to show that you're fully qualified."

He began to shut the door, but with a gesture of despair the young man stopped him. "I could break sticks," he cried.

"Sticks!" the Devil cried. And he laughed, a wild laugh like the neighing of a million hyenas. "Sticks! Hell's bells, man, the fires here have been burning for eternity. We never need sticks."

And he banged the door in the young man's face.

The young man was in absolute despair. Nobody wanted him on Earth because he had no experience, and nobody wanted him in either Heaven or Hell. He didn't know what to do. He knew of nowhere else he could go.

And so he began to float about in limbo. And he found plenty of people there to keep him company, people who had made a mess of their lives or people who couldn't fit into the scheme of things at all. They floated about, weeping and moaning and wringing their hands, singing a chorus of *What are we to do? To do? We have got no experience, Yes, we've got no experience, got no experience to-day!*

Soon the young man got heartily sick of them. They could not help it, poor devils, but they got on his nerves. He got fed up seeing them floating past him with their wan white faces, their thin hands clutching their bellies in their efforts to make the hunger-pangs go away. "I can't stand this any longer," he said, and he decided to return to Earth. Perhaps by this time somebody would have died and created a vacancy for him.

But when he returned to his former existence he found that things were just as bad as they had been before. In fact, they were worse. There was a war on. And before he knew where he was the young man was dragged into it.

He protested vigorously. "But I'm a Pacifist," he cried to the soldiers amongst whom he found himself marching.

"That doesn't matter a damn," they said. "You've jolly well got to fight or be killed."

"But what are you fighting for?" he demanded. "I've been away from the Earth for so long that I don't know which side is which. They all look pretty much alike to me."

"They all look pretty much alike to us, too," they said. "But that doesn't matter. What does matter is that you've got to blare away at whatever *they* tell you."

"At whatever *who* tells you?"

"The high-head ones," they said. "Those that make the wars and tell us to fight them. Here's one of them coming just now."

A sergeant-major was approaching. The young man could hardly believe his eyes when he saw him. It was the grocer at the end of the street where the young man used to live. He was a particularly surly man who gave short measure and wouldn't give "tick." The young man gaped so much that he went out of step and tripped over his feet, an action that immediately singled him out for the sergeant-major's notice.

"Company, halt!" he cried.

He swaggered up to the young man and examined him from top to toe. "Hm, a new recruit," he said. "A very poor specimen, too. Can't even put on his uniform properly. The poor dear's missing his valet!"

The soldiers laughed dutifully.

"Where's your rifle?" the sergeant-major snapped.

The young man shrugged. "I dunno."

"Call me ' sir '," the sergeant-major roared.

"Isn't that your place?" the young man said sarcastically. "I thought you always addressed your customers as 'sir.'"

"None of your insolence," the sergeant-major cried." "You're just too funny. It's a good job that I'm a soft-hearted bloke. If you said that to one of the regular officers it would have been the firing-squad for you."

"Well, hurry up and get it over with," the young man said wearily. "I'm tired of living. I'd be better dead. Really dead this time."

"Oh, you'll die quick enough," the sergeant-major said. "But not as easily as all that. First you've got to try to kill somebody yourself."

"But I don't want to kill anybody."

"Chicken-hearted, eh?" the sergeant-major sneered. "You rookies! What you need is a nurse-maid."

"You're right, sergie old boy!" cried a voice from the rear ranks.

This time the laughter wasn't dutiful. The sergeant-major was furious. "Here," he cried, thrusting a rifle into the young man's hands. "Get that over your shoulder and march. We're going into the front line."

"But I don't know how to use it," the young man protested.

The sergeant-major laughed sarcastically.

"I haven't had any experience," the young man said.

The sergeant-major laughed again, and his laughter was worse than the high, mad neighing of the Devil. It was like the roaring of billions of bloodthirsty jackals, eager for blood.

"No experience!" he cried. "That doesn't matter. We'll bloody soon see that you get some!"

10. BLACKOUT

He was going to kiss Joan when her mother popped her head around the living-room door.

"Oh, it's you, Stanley!" she cried. "I thought it was Aunt Maggie."

Stanley grinned with embarrassment and took his arm away from Joan. "It's me," he said.

"Come away in," Mrs. Stuart said. "Isn't it awful?"

"Awful," Stanley agreed.

"Hello, Stanley!" Mr. Stuart looked up from his newspaper. "I thought you'd have been away to Poland!"

Stanley grinned. He sat down on the sofa and carefully pulled up his trousers so as not to disturb the knife-edged crease. And he swung round his gas-mask and placed it on his knee. "Nuisance carrying those things!" he said, his fingers smoothing the edges of the smart blue leather case.

"We'll just have to put up with them," Mr. Stuart said. "We've got to put up with an awful lot in this world. We can't always get our own way, y'know!"

"Aren't you going to take off your raincoat?" Mrs. Stuart said.

"It's not worth my while," he said. "Joan and I are going out."

"Well, you can't go just yet," Mrs. Stuart said. "I want Joan to help me put up the curtains for the Blackout first." She sighed heavily. "Isn't it awful? We'll soon not be able to call our lives our own. All those rules and regulations. What's your mother saying to it? Has she got all her windows darkened properly?"

"I think so," Stanley said.

"I don't know what we're going to do if this war lasts three years. Goodness! We'll all be driven mad by that time. Five days have been bad enough."

Joan sat down on the sofa beside Stanley. She slipped her hand into his arm, smiling at him. He pressed her hand against his side, wishing he had had time to kiss her.

"Hello, Stanley!" Joan's fifteen-year-old brother, Bill, came whistling from the back garden. "Not in uniform yet?"

"No." Stanley smiled, conscious that his neck was flushed.

"You'll have to go sooner or later," Mr. Stuart said, lowering his paper. "It's a pity, but..... We all have to do our bit, y'know."

"I guess so," Stanley said.

"This 'll ruin your career, won't it?" Mrs. Stuart said, and Stanley thought that he detected a complacent note in her voice. "You won't be going back to the 'Varsity, will you?"

"Well, I don't know...."

"Of course, he won't," Mr. Stuart said firmly. "The 'Varsity won't be opening. There won't be any students. There 'll be only girls, and most of them will be doing work of National Service, anyway."

"But all the young men aren't being called up," Mrs. Stuart protested. "Mr. Chamberlain said....."

"Ah, it won't be long." Mr. Stuart pressed tobacco firmly into the bowl of his pipe. "Another week or two and every man of military age will be in uniform. Just wait until they get things organised." And he struck a match decisively and held it to his pipe.

Stanley looked at Joan, but she was watching her father. He looked down at the tips of his light tan shoes. It's all very well for him to talk, he thought. He's well over fifty and he knows that there's no danger of Bill having to go; the war'll be over by the time he's eighteen.

"It's getting dark," Mrs. Stuart said. "Will you help me with those curtains now, Joan?"

Mrs. Stuart closed the windows and pulled the blinds. Then she pulled the curtains. "Now, Joan," she said. The two women stood at either end of the window and lifted a roller from the floor. They held it while they stepped gingerly on chairs and held it above the window. They unwound the blanket that was rolled around it, and immediately the room was plunged into pitch-darkness.

"Put on the light now, Bill," said Mrs. Stuart.

Bill fell over something on his way to the switch, and he muttered a schoolboyish curse. "Don't let me hear you say that again, young man," his father said when the light went on. "Remember you're not in the army—yet!" And he looked at Stanley and laughed.

"This is just a makeshift arrangement, of course," Mrs. Stuart nodded at the blanket. "Goodness knows we'll have to get something easier than this if this war is going to last."

"I should hope so," said Joan. "You can't expect me to stay in every night and help you with it."

"Well, you'll just have to put up with it in the meantime," Mrs. Stuart said sharply. "Where can you want to go, anyway? I'm sure you can't go anywhere at nights. All the picture-houses and dance-halls are closed."

"But they won't stay closed all the time," Joan mumbled.

"Won't they?" Mrs. Stuart snorted. Then she smiled at Stanley's gloomy face. "Well, we'll hope not! Come on, Joan, help me with the upstairs windows."

Stanley stared from the smoke of his cigarette to the tips of his shoes. Mr. Stuart puffed smoke from behind his paper. Bill slouched to the door. "I'm away," he said, and he closed the door after him. "Don't be late," Mr. Stuart called, without looking up from his paper.

When she came downstairs Mrs. Stuart poked at the blanket over the living-room window, re-arranging the curtains at the sides. "I hope that's all right," she said. "I don't want any of these Air-Raid Wardens to come and complain about it."

"Oh, it's fine," Mr. Stuart said, giving it a brief glance.

"Listen to him!" exclaimed his wife. "A lot of help he is! Every light in the house could be blazing and not a curtain drawn, yet he wouldn't move off that chair to do anything about it!"

"Why should I?"

"Huh, you'd move quick enough if the German aeroplanes came over," Mrs. Stuart said scornfully.

She touched the blanket again. "I wonder if it's all right?" she said in a worried voice. "You might go out and have a look, Joan."

"We'll both go," Stanley said, rising quickly.

"Nonsense!" said Mrs. Stuart. "Just you sit where you are."

Stanley resumed his seat sulkily. He wished that Joan would hurry up and go out with him. If they didn't hurry up, all the best seats in the park would be bagged. All the fellows and girls that he knew were saying what a great war it was. They were having the time of their lives in the Blackout.

"There's a chink down the right-hand side," Joan said, returning from her inspection of the windows.

"There's a chink in your head!" Mrs. Stuart said irritably, and she tugged at the curtain. "See if that'll do."

Stanley made to rise and follow Joan outside, but Mr. Stuart said suddenly: "I see that they're wanting men in the R.A.M.C., Stanley. Stretcher-bearers and such-like. There's your chance."

Stanley grinned. "Well—I—er—"

"Of course, you maybe think a stretcher-bearer's beneath you," Mr. Stuart said. "But it's a chance to do something worth while."

"Well, I—I think I'll wait a bit," Stanley said, putting his forefinger between his collar and his neck. "I don't want to rush into things."

"You'd be safe enough in the R.A.M.C.," Mr. Stuart said, and he looked at Stanley over the top of his newspaper, smiling a little.

"You're not safe anywhere!" Stanley laughed and stood up. "Nearly ready?" he said to Joan.

"We won't go just yet," she said. "We'll wait until Aunt Maggie comes. We haven't seen her since the war started. I'm just gasping to hear what she has to say about it all. She's sure to have someting funny to say. You know what a scream she is!"

"Uhuh," Stanley said, slowly sitting down again.

Joan sat down beside him. "Aunt Maggie's a perfect yell," she said. "I wouldn't miss her for anything."

Stanley said nothing. He scraped his thumbnail over a spot on his trousers, wondering where the spot had come from.

"There's the gate!" cried Mrs. Stuart. "That'll be Aunt Maggie now."

Joan ran to open the door. Stanley heard her shrill little squeaks of greeting being swamped by Aunt Maggie's deep-bosomed bombardment in the hall. He fixed a smile on his face and looked at the door.

"Isn't it awful?" Aunt Maggie cried.

"Isn't it terrible?" cried Mrs. Stuart.

Aunt Maggie sat down beside Stanley, her huge bulk spreading over the sofa so that he was forced to squeeze into his corner. He looked disconsolately at Joan, but she was sitting on the edge of a chair, leaning forward with her elbows on her knees, looking eagerly at her aunt.

"My word!" Aunt Maggie loosened the high collar of her coat, and her three chins, released from their bondage, shook like a balloon-barrage. "It's hot, isn't it? The hottest September I can remember for a while. What grand holiday weather it would have been if only this old war hadn't been on!"

"Yes, it's hard lines on those who had fixed their holidays late," Mr. Stuart said complacently. He had had his holiday in July.

"It's fair upset everything," Aunt Maggie declared, unbuttoning her coat, and with the loosening of every button, appearing to get bigger and bigger. "It's a terrible nuisance. That Hitler has a lot to answer for."

"I'd just like to get my hands on him," Mrs. Stuart said vindictively. "If he only knew the bother he was putting folk to! All this Blackout.... How are you managing, Maggie?"

"Managing!" Aunt Maggie snorted as she took off her hat and stuck the hat-pins violently into the crown. "My word, you never saw such a carry-on as we have every night. Jumping up and down, fastening curtains and blinds. And then you've no sooner got them up and you think they're O.K. than some blasted Air-Raid Warden knocks at your door and says there's a light and would you kindly look into it."

"A light!" she exclaimed. "My word, I've been sore put to it not to put out some of their lights! It took me all my time not to flatten two young whippersnappers of policemen who came to our door last night. Excuse me, they says, there's a light showing. Excuse me!" Aunt Maggie mimicked their polite accents. "I was fair boiling," she said. "After me spending the best part of half-an-hour darkening all the windows, determined that they wouldn't be able to find any fault. It's fair aggravating."

"It is that," said Mrs. Stuart.

"I just hope that *that* Hitler has as much bother as he's giving us," Aunt Maggie said. "If I hear right, there's so many windows in Bertie's Garden that he'll have a sad job putting up and taking down the curtains."

"Pity he wouldn't spend all his time at it then," sniffed Mrs. Stuart. "If only he'd do that instead of upsetting folk."

Aunt Maggie sighed. "Ah well, I suppose we'll get more than that to bother us by and by. Just wait till the air-raids start!"

"Did you hear the warning on Sunday?" Mrs. Stuart leaned forward, almost whispering as though it were some secret that the Ministry of Information had ordered not to be divulged.

"I did that!" Aunt Maggie laughed. "My word, you'd have got your kill if you'd been in our house on Sunday forenoon. We were all having our breakfast when Mr. Chamberlain gave his speech. A real good speech, wasn't it? Poor man, I felt that sorry for him having to say what he had to say. Especially on a Sunday. I don't see why that Hitler always picks Sundays to do his bad deeds on. You'd think he'd let folk have their Sundays in peace."

Aunt Maggie rose and began to peel off her coat. Stanley assisted her. "Thanks, Stanley," she said, sitting down again. "Well, when Mr. Chamberlain stopped speaking I went up the stairs to make the beds. Tommy was in his pyjamas and his dressing-gown, and he started to wash the dishes. I had just got our bed made and I was making Tommy's when I heard the sirens. Goodness me, I couldn't believe it. I just stood there like a big tattiebogle and listened. Then I heard Tommy come bounding up the stairs. 'It's an air-raid, ma,' he cried, and he off with his dressing-gown and pulls a pair of breeks over his pyjamas. 'Get away,' I says. 'It can't be an air-raid. They haven't had time to come across yet.' But down the stairs I goes with my handbag and the wee case where I keep all my insurance policies. I goes out to the back door and there I sees Father going into the Shelter with a fifty box of Gold Flake and two bottles of stout."

Aunt Maggie laughed heartily at the recollection. "He was determined to pass out in style, anyway," she said. "'My word,' I says to him, 'You're fairly looking after yourself.' Well, I handed him my bags and I was going to creep into the shelter when I thought maybe I'd better get a coat. I was just wearing an overall, and if the house was going to be knocked down, I didn't want to go about the street wearing that."

"You should have had one of these Siren Ensembles!" Mrs. Stuart laughed.

"That's what Tommy said. He said, 'You'll have to get an Emergency Gown, ma!'" Aunt Maggie giggled. "My word, if I had they would have so much bother fastening me into it that the bombers would be over before we knew where we were."

"Tommy's a great lad," said Mrs. Stuart. "He's always so cheerful, poor laddie. It's a wonder he can keep so cheery, him with his weak chest.'"

"It is that," said his mother. "He really was terribly funny that forenoon. He came out of the back-door, carrying the bird's cage, and singing that song *Tina*. You know the one! My word, you'd have died if you'd heard him singing: 'Tina, soon the bombs will be falling, and Adolf will be calling, It's a sad melody!'"

"Fancy him remembering the bird," Mrs. Stuart said sentimentally.

"Yes, that put the peter on things," said Aunt Maggie. "Father came out of the shelter then. 'For the love o' God,' he says. 'Take that cage back into the house again. There's time enough to bother about the bird when the air-raid starts.'"

She wiped the tears of laughter from her eyes. "It was terrible funny," she said. "We were all running about like a lot of mad folk and not a single aeroplane to be seen! That's what the man next door said. They didn't hear the warning at all, so Tommy hammered on their door and cried, 'It's an air-raid.' But when Mr. McLaren popped his head out of the top window—he had been asleep, poor man—he looked up at the sky and said, 'It can't be; I don't hear the anti-aircraft guns.'"

They were all helpless with laughter. Stanley squirmed and thought: If I hear the words *that Hitler* again, I'll scream. It's the new hymn of hate, dinned into everybody by the papers and the wireless.

"Wasn't it funny?" Aunt Maggie nudged him in the ribs, leaning over him and laughing so that he got the impression that her well-upholstered bulk was oozing over him and going to swamp him.

"Yes," he said, and he forced a grin.

"What did you do when you heard the warning?"

"Nothing," he said. "I didn't hear it."

"Didn't hear it?" She stared at him. "But surely—?"

"I was in bed," he said. "It didn't wake me up."

"In bed?" Aunt Maggie's mouth opened so widely that the lines between her three chins became even more prominent. "But weren't you up to hear Mr. Chamberlain?"

"No." He smiled and shrugged.

"But goodness gracious!" she cried. "It was a historic occasion."

"I guess so," he said. "But what was the good of listening? We knew what he was going to say, anyway."

Aunt Maggie sighed and turned to Mr. Stuart. "Really, those young ones, they don't seem to realize. But you'll realize all right when you get into the army," she added cheerfully. "My word, you'll get smartened up there!"

Stanley tried to smile distantly as though to say that the army was still a good bit away and that lots of things might happen before then. Aunt Maggie looked him up and down critically.

"There's no danger of them not taking you," she said. "I'd just need to look at you to pass you A.1."

"Tommy and I must get into the same regiment!" Stanley laughed, wondering if his laughter sounded as hollow to them as it did to himself.

"Oh, they won't take Tommy," Aunt Maggie said. "Poor laddie, he's not strong at all. They'd never *dare* to pass him."

"Of course not," Mrs. Stuart said decisively. "He could never be passed with his weak chest. The very idea!"

"Well?" Stanley looked at Joan. "Are you ready to go now?"

She smiled and stood up. But her parents protested at once. "Don't be silly," Mrs. Stuart said. "Where can you go, anyway?"

"We're just going for a walk," Stanley said.

"You're going for no walk at this time of night," Mrs. Stuart said.

"But, Mummy—" Joan cried.

"The idea!" said Mrs. Stuart.

"You'll stay where you are," said Mr. Stuart sternly. "Going out in this blackout. It's preposterous. You can't see a foot in front of you."

"But there are plenty of people out," Stanley said, thinking of the giggling and shuffling he had heard as he passed the park.

"A lot of guisers!" said Mr. Stuart.

"My word, yes, some of these young folk are having the time of their lives!" Aunt Maggie laughed. "There's no knowing what mischief some of them are up to! I just wish there had been a Blackout when I was young!"

"Help me to set the supper, Joan," said her mother.

Aunt Maggie prattled on cheerily about the laxity of this generation's morals, and occasionally Mr. Stuart grunted agreement from behind his paper. Stanley said nothing.

All through supper Mrs. Stuart and her sister talked about food-rationing and the prices the shops were charging for blackout curtain material. "Profiteering!" cried Mrs. Stuart. Hearing the sound of the wireless from next door, Mr. Stuart put on theirs. They hummed and beat their feet in time with a crooner singing:

The richest in the land, the poorest of us all,
We must all stick together,
Birds of a feather.
And the clouds will soon roll by!

Stanley tried to catch Joan's feet between his own under the table, but he stopped when Aunt Maggie looked roguishly at him and cried: "Oh, my corns!"

Stanley rose as soon as supper was over. "I think I'd better go," he said.

"Yes, it doesn't do to stay out too late these nights," Mrs. Stuart said. "Home's the best place these days."

Stanley stood at the living-room door and bade them a general good-night. Joan was waiting for him in the lobby. "I expect you'll have on your uniform the next time we see you," Mr. Stuart said.

Stanley laughed and said: "Maybe."

He attempted to shut the living-room door after him, but Mrs. Stuart followed him into the lobby. She opened the front door at once. The lobby was so narrow that Joan had to stand behind her mother, out of Stanley's reach. "We'd better not stand at the door," Mrs. Stuart said. "In case any light shows out. Good night."

"Good night," Stanley said, and he looked despairingly at Joan.

The chink of light was snapped suddenly, and the door banged, leaving him in complete darkness. He stumbled against the edge of the flower-bed as he began to grope his way towards the gate. "Damn!" he muttered. And as he clicked the gate behind him and started to feel his way along the street, he could hear laughter and the blare of martial music coming from behind all the darkened windows, mocking him.

11. NOT SO PRETTY POLLY

Polly spat down into the back-green. Sir Lancelot was running in the three-thirty and she hadn't a damned tosser to back him with. She leaned her elbows on the window-sill; her wrinkled old face glowered at the back of the tenement opposite. A strand of her coarse frizzy red hair dangled in front of her eyes, tickling her nose. She blew irritably at it, but it still dangled. She spat again into the back-green, just missing the patched shirt and torn towels that were hanging out of the window beneath.

She'd got to have something on Sir Lancelot. She always won off him. And the Whittington Stakes was always a lucky race with her. Prunella, Red Stardust, Fancy Free. . . . . the names of past winners of the Whittington Stakes, which she had backed, crowded into her memory. Lord love a duck, she must have something on. This was the first year she had missed having a bet on this race.

But her bets had been getting fewer and fewer lately. Her luck seemed to have run out. There was nobody she could dun for money now, except Dickyboy. Her red-rimmed little eyes glinted. Dickyboy was a lad and a half. He'd be along tonight as usual. Every Saturday night as regular as clockwork he came along for his bit of fun. Tee hee, he was a one! He wasn't much to look at with his bandy legs and heavy belly, but when he came in and put his hand on her..... Polly sniggered and a shudder of delight passed through her shrunken body. They said there were no fools like old fools. Well, she and Dickyboy could show a lot of those young whippersnappers a thing or two.

She slip-slopped away from the window. Her stockinged-feet kicked against an empty beer bottle, and she cursed. She could raise twopence on those, anyway, she thought, putting it beside another empty bottle standing among the ashes in the fireplace. She looked about, but everything that could be pawned in the slovenly attic had been pawned long ago. She sat down on the unmade bed with its assortment of rags, and she placed her head on her hands, thinking.

She'd got to raise the wind somehow. It was meat and drink for her to have a bet on. And especially on Sir Lancelot. She hadn't fancied a horse so much since Pretty Polly. Lord love a duck, but that was a long time ago! The first horse she had ever backed. She's been a pretty Polly herself then. She cackled, her toothless gums gaping at the remembrance.

She reached under the bed and took out her basket. Nothing there that she could hope to sell. Since the war people were getting that they always took something out of the basket. The days were past when they gave her a penny or twopence and said they wouldn't bother taking anything to-day, thank you. Since the war people were getting greedy. Either that or they didn't feel as sorry for her as they had once done. The number of times that disgusted faces banged the door on her.....

She kicked the basket back under the bed. There was nothing else for it but Woollies. She cursed her creaking joints as she pulled on her shauchled old shoes and put on her old raincoat. Then, picking up the two empty bottles, she locked the door behind her and felt her way down the dark dirty stair.

Two or three children were playing in the court. As soon as they saw her they began to chant " Polly, put my....." But they ran, their voices still singing the obscene parody, fading into the noise of the traffic in the High Street.

Polly muttered angrily to herself as she trotted on her short legs across the High Street and down the Fleshmarket Close. Her hands in her pockets, her red head lolling on her shoulders, she cursed the children and the weather, Dickyboy and the hard pavements. It was a hell of a world when a poor old body couldn't get enough money for a bet. She drittled into a licensed grocer's shop and planked down the two bottles. Trauchling down Market Street, the sight of the clock on the N.B. Station Hotel reminded her that she didn't have much time. Twelve o'clock.

Snailing through Woolworth's, she had every nerve on the alert. She had done this so often that she knew every move. She pushed through the crowd milling around the Haberdashery counter. The two assistants were busy serving. Polly began to rake among the cards of hair-nets. She clutched the twopence she had got for the beer bottles. It was safer to have money with you. Beside her a young woman with hair dyed redder than Polly's own, swaying dangerously on too-high heels, was examining Sanitary Belts. She was dressed in black; a black saucer-like hat sat precariously on her forehead, held in place by a black velvet band. She sniffed disdainfully and edged away from the old woman. Polly grinned with toothless maliciousness. Tee hee, lord love a duck, the high and mighty miss didn't know what lay before her. Polly knew what she was, trust Polly! She remembered when she had been like that herself. Maybe she'd be driven to pinching out of Woollies, too, in time. You never knew. When you got older and you got a craving for something, there was no knowing what lengths it might drive you to. The craving to bet was stronger than the craving for drink. Polly knew because she had both.

"Ony red hair-nets, hen?" she said in a familiar tone to one of the assistants. "I'm goin' to meet ma lad the night, and I want to look ma best." She turned and grinned at the young woman.

The assistant fumbled in the pile. "I'll see if we have any along here," she said, going to the end of the counter and looking under it. Polly took the opportunity to push several cards of hair-nets up her sleeve. "It's a' richt, hen," she called. "Dinnie bother."

She moved along the counter, pushing in to rake among the garter elastic and the cards of Dinkie Curlers. Under her sandy brows her small red-rimmed eyes were on the watch. She did not need to watch her hands; they were well trained in their work. Still, used though she was, she tingled with excitement. At any minute a hand might fall on her shoulder, or somebody might accuse her. The other shoppers weren't to be trusted.

At last she thought: Enough's as good as a feast. And she moved away to the Toilet Requisites counter. Sniffing the cakes of soap, she managed to secrete two of them in her sleeve. She moved on with seeming carelessness, her red head lolling on the shoulders of her dirty coat: a small drab figure slipping unobtrusively through the crowds. She made for the nearest exit. If she just got out safely now, everything would be okay.

Two little girls with a dog on a leash were between her and the door. The dog was in Polly's way; it had its leg cocked up against the corner of a counter.

" See here," Polly rebuked them. " Ye shouldnie .let yer dog dae that in here."

In an entry in West Register Street, she examined her spoils. Four hair-nets, two cakes of soap, two cards of garter elastic and two cards of Dinkie Curlers. She'd seen the day when she might have done better. But Saturday was a bad day; there were so many busybodies in Woollies, moving about, ready to pounce on you. It wasn't only the shop-walkers and the assistants you had to watch. Some people had too little to do.

Polly decided not to bother going home for her basket. She speculated one of her pennies on a tram-ride into the suburbs. By pretending that she was dozing she managed to get a two-penny ride. " It's a grand day, son," she said cheerfully to the conductor as she got off. " It's a hap-hap-happy day!" she skirled. Her red-gummed mouth gaped and she gave him a dunch with her bony elbow. " It'll be fine the night for wenching!"

She entered a street of little bungalows strung together like beads, with red and grey tiled roofs alternately. Her mouth dropped in an expression of dejection and she pushed open the first gate.

"Are ye needin' ony elastic, missis?" she whined, holding out her wares. "Or ony soap? It's awfu' cheap. Only twopence ..."

"I'm sorry." The door banged in her face.

She muttered under her breath as she went down the path, and she left the gate open behind her. A young man opened the next door and her spirits went up; men were always easier to deal with.

"Is yer missis wantin' ony elastic, son? Or hair-nets?" She held them out enticingly. "Ye wouldnie like to buy her one, would ye, son? They're awfu' cheap."

"Well—er—" The young man took a step backward. "I don't know whether she—Mother!" he called.

"Tell her we don't want anything," said a loud shrewish voice.

"I'm—er—sorry," he stammered.

"Ye havenie got a wee drop dinner left over, have ye?" Polly said wheedlingly. "I havenie had a bite for twa days, that's honest."

"Come in and shut the door," the shrewish voice called. "Don't waste time with her."

The young man grinned in a sickly way. He looked over his shoulder, his hand in his trousers-pocket. "I'm awfully sorry," he said, "but we don't need anything." And as he shut the door he put a threepenny-bit into Polly's ready hand.

The woman at the next house bought a cake of soap for twopence. "Though I'll probably never use it," she said. "The last cake I bought at the door was so hard that I was terrified I'd skin my face."

But Polly had no luck at the next two houses; the doors were banged in her face, one housewife adding insult to injury by calling her "a stinking old besom."

In gates hopefully, out of them disconsolately, Polly went up one side of the street. Coming down the other side more often than not there was no answer to her repeated knocks. The occupants had seen her going up, and most of them had not the courage to come and say "No, thank you." Polly knew that most of them were in, because she heard wirelesses, and occasionally she saw people peering from behind curtains. She was furious; she chattered to herself like an angry chimpanzee, and she left a trail of open gates behind her.

Fivepence! She spat at the end of the street. A clock chimed. Would that be one or half-past? She quickened her pace and went into the next street which was identical with the first one. Out of one bungalow into the next.....
She shut three gates behind her. And at the end of the street she had sold one hair-net, and she had tenpence—elevenpence that was, counting the penny from the other bottle, which she would need to pay her car back to town.

She must get at least another twopence. It was two o'clock. Lord love a duck, she would need to hurry up! She managed quite easily to get tears into the corners of her red-rimmed eyes "Can ye help a puir auld body, missis?" she whined. "I havenie had a bite for three days and I must get enough to pay for ma bed the night."

The young woman who had opened the door, thrust back the child who was peering around her skirts. "Well, I don't really need anything," she said in an uncertain tone.

Polly realized at once that here was somebody whose sympathies could be worked upon. "Aw, ye're surely needin' somethin'," she pleaded. "Hair-nets? Soap? Elastic? A bonnie young lassie like you will aye be needin' elastic." She tittered bawdily. "I ken what men are and how hard they are on elastic when they begin to get......" She leered; then bending down she simpered at the child: "Hello, hen, are ye havin' a holiday the day? Or is she no' auld enough to be at the school?"

"She's just four," the woman said.

"Ay, she's big for her age," Polly said. "I could 'a' sworn she was six. She's a fine big healthy lassie. Aren't ye, dearie? Eh, I wish I was a bairn again. I never thought when I was that age that I'd be driven to this. No' kennin' where ma next meal's comin' frae."

"I'll take those curlers," the young woman said.

While her mother was inside, the child peered fearfully at Polly. The old woman held out her hand enticingly, but the child did not move. She did not even smile when Polly gave a few skips to entertain her. She stared blankly at the old drab's antics.

" There's a sixpence," the woman said. " Just keep the change."

" Ah, ye've got a kind heart, dearie," Polly said. " I hope ye'll be rewarded for it. But ye will, I know ye will. God's good to us all. God bless ye both," she added piously.

.On the journey back in the tram she debated what she would do with her one and fourpence. She still had one pair of Dinkie Curlers, one cake of soap, two cards of elastic and three hair-nets left, but they would keep for another day. She must get back to be in time for Jackie, the bookie's runner. He would be at the corner of St. Giles at three o'clock. She decided to buy two pies for herself and Dickyboy with the fourpence. The shilling would go on Sir Lancelot. Should she put sixpence each way, or should she put it all on for a win? But she didn't need to worry about that. Lord love a duck, Sir Lancelot had never let her down yet.

At twenty past three she put a shilling for a win on Sir Lancelot and slip-slopped home to prepare for Dickyboy.

12. THE SAND OF DUNKIRK

It was astonishing the amount of sand the soldiers brought aboard with them. They had sand in their boots, sand in their knapsacks, sand in the seams of their trousers, sand in their hair. Sand seemed to slide off them from the unlikeliest places. Soon the whole deck was covered with it.

"Talk about the blinkin' Sahara!" the second mate said. "I haven't seen as much sand since I was a kid playin' with my spade and pail at Portobello."

"You can have my share of it," the skipper said. "I don't want to see any more sand as long as I live."

"Well, maybe that won't be so long," the second said. "If this rammy keeps on."

"Ay, you're right."

The skipper eased the chin-strap of his steel-helmet and gave his shoulders a wriggle. Sand seemed to be sliding down his spine along with the sweat. "This is a bit too hot for me," he said.

"Reminds me of the searchlight tattoo I once saw," the second said.

"Searchlight tattoo my foot!" the skipper said. "What searchlight tattoo ever had bombs and live shells bursting around!"

He leaned on the rail of the bridge and watched the soldiers coming up the gangway. "God knows where they're all coming from," he said. There was an apparently never-ending stream of stretchers each carried by four soldiers, most of whom were wounded and exhausted. "Where are we going to put them all?"

"We'll get them stowed some place," the second said. "They won't mind where they're put so long as they get away from Dunkirk."

"By God, I wish we were loaded and away." The skipper lit a cigarette and puffed it nervously.

"Don't we all?" the second said. "I'll away down and see how they're gettin' on."

He was going down the companionway when a shell burst less than fifty yards from the pier. He whistled and eased the neck of his polo-sweater. That was too near for his taste. "Are there many more to come?" he asked a sergeant standing at the top of the gangway.

"Thousands."

The sergeant took a stub of cigarette from behind his ear and put it in his mouth. "Give us a light, Mac!"

The second held out his cigarette. The sergeant put out his hand and held it against his own cigarette. "You're shakin', Mac!"

"Who isn't?"

The second turned away and looked at the human cargo. They were lying everywhere, packing themselves into every available inch of space. If we get any more, he thought, the old tub'll burst. Stretchers, wounded and exhausted men, they were piled higgledy-piggledy on top of each other. Some of them were already asleep. They were on a boat and they didn't give a damn what happened to them now. Already in their minds they were away from the inferno of Dunkirk. They were on the sea, and they remembered that Britannia ruled the waves.

"We can't take many more," he said to the sergeant. "We're overloaded as it is."

The sergeant took a quick glance over the decks. "Oh, we can squeeze in another thirty, anyway." He leaned over the side and called to the patient mass of khaki on the quay: "Only another thirty, boys, and they'd better all be wounded."

The second went up on the bridge and told the skipper they could prepare to sail. "Not before time," the skipper said. "Any minute here may be our last. I'm gettin' windy."

"You're gettin'!" the second said. "I am, and I've been for a while."

He looked at the smoke rising from the fires in the town, lying above the dull red glow like huge, evil black and grey blossoms. If this happened in Leith . . . . . If his young wife had to flee with a bundle as he had seen the refugees flying from Dunkirk . . . . .

In less than a quarter of an hour they were nosing their way past the other vessels waiting to collect troops. The second looked anxiously upwards. If only they could get away safely before another fleet of German bombers swooped down from the clouds. God, but he'd be glad to see New-haven harbour!

The mate had been trying to snatch a few minutes rest. When he came on the bridge, the skipper told the second to go and get something to eat. "Okay, I'm needin' it badly," the second said. "Chocolate and cigarettes are hardly the sort o' stuff heroes should be fed on!"

"Heroes!" The skipper laughed and aimed a kick at him.

The second went below, grinning. In two or three minutes, he popped his head up the companionway. "Come down and see this, skipper!"

A crowd of soldiers were milling around the galley. The steward and the galley-boy were handing out cups of tea. A long queue was waiting patiently to be served. The skipper stood and watched for a few minutes, then he edged his way through the crowd. "Excuse me a minute, boys," he said, entering the galley.

"What's this?" he said to the steward.

He jerked his thumb at a half-open drawer of a cupboard. It was almost full of coins. He looked from the drawer to the steward and picked up one of the coins.

"Francs!" he said.

"Well, I thought I'd charge them a franc a cup," the steward said aggressively. "They're damned glad to get it at any price."

"They get it for nothing on this boat," the skipper said. He made a swift movement and pulled out the drawer. The steward's face flushed a brick-red as the skipper carried the drawer past him.

"Here—" he said.

"This is where they're going, and you should be bloody glad I'm not sending you after them," the skipper said, and he strode to the side and threw the drawer and its contents overboard. "If I hear of you taking another franc I'll . . . ."

He frowned and went back to the bridge. The second cocked a snook at the steward and followed the skipper. They leaned on the rail of the bridge and looked down at the soldiers still trying to rid themselves of the sand; and the skipper told the mate what had happened. "But that's settled his hash," he said. They looked at each other and nodded. And they smiled as the boat ploughed its way steadily nearer and nearer to the coast of England.

13. MAN ABOUT THE HOUSE

When Mrs. Watt opened the gate she saw a fair-haired young man watching her out of the window. Waddling up the path, she was aware of him watching her every step. The road from the bus-stop had been uphill, and the sweat was trickling down her forehead and fat blowsy cheeks. She wiped her face, and as she drew her fingers across her brow, she saw that the young man was still standing at the window, gazing at her. As if he were staring at something in the zoo, she thought. She went to the back door, and as she was raising her hand to knock, the young man opened the door suddenly. She stood with her upraised hand in the air, feeling foolish.

" You'll be the new charwoman?" he said.

She nodded and shuffled past him.

" My mother's not up yet," he said. " But you can just begin."

She put her black oilskin bag on the chair in the scullery and as she unpinned her hat she took stock of him. He was a very pale young man with hollow cheeks pitted with huge pores. He had pale blue, watery eyes that stared persistently at her from between his almost white lashes. She felt vaguely uncomfortable under his stare as she took her apron out of her bag and tied it around her fat stomach.

" What do you want me to do first? " she said.

" You can do the fires," he said.

He showed her the box with blacklead and brushes. " You know how to clean a fire, don't you?" he said. " You rake out the ashes and you take away the fender and———"

Mrs. Watt laughed. " Bless me, laddie!" she said. " I cleaned fireplaces long before ye were born."

He stood and watched her as she set to work. All the time she was blackleading she was conscious of his watchful pale eyes, and she began to be annoyed at his continued scrutiny. He had to step aside when she took out the ashes to the bin, and she said: " Ye're like my first joker, he was aye gettin' in the way. I often used to say to him, 'G'wa oot o' ma road for ony favour and let me get on wi' ma work'."

But the young man did not take the hint. He hovered about the room, moving restlessly from one chair to another. He kept up a persistent breathing through his half-open mouth. It was neither a whistle nor a tune and it began to get on Mrs. Watt's nerves.

" What'll I do next? " she said.

" The dishes."

He went before her into the scullery and pointed to a pile of dirty dishes on the board by the sink. " You know how to do them, don't you?" he said. " You drip them on this tray."

Mrs. Watt laughed, but she did not say anything. The laddie's surely sort of simple, she said to herself. But she knitted her brows irritably when he lounged against the boiler and watched her. He was behind her, but all the time she was aware of the thin, tuneless whistling. She rattled the dishes noisily, trying to vent her irritation on them. She was relieved when Mrs. Laurie came in. She was a tired-looking little woman with a fretful face and pale eyes like her son.

" Good morning, Mrs. Watt," she said. " Has Eric been telling you what to do? "

" Ay," Mrs. Watt said.

" I don't know what I'd do without him," Mrs. Laurie said. " He's such a comfort to me. Far better than many a daughter would have been. He's terribly handy about the house."

"I can see that," Mrs. Watt said.

Mrs. Laurie leaned against the sink and began to lament about her troubles. Not that Mrs. Watt could see that she had any cause to complain. Her husband, who had been a well-to-do market gardener, had died several years before, and had left her in very comfortable circumstances.

"Eric was our only child," she said. "He's all that I've got left now. Thank goodness, he's never needed to go out and work. I don't know what I'd have done if he'd had to go out every day to business. For all that he would have made, anyway. It wouldn't have been worth it. And I feel that I need somebody to keep me company. It's nice, I always think, to have a man about the house."

"Well, it depends on the man," Mrs. Watt said. "I've had three, and none o' them were the kind o' men that ye like to see sittin' continually by the fireside. No' that that kept them frae doin' that, of course. None o' them were the kind that would break their necks bein' in the front o' ony queue lookin' for work. My first joker especially. Bless me, but he was oftener at hame than he was in a job."

She sighed as she polished the chairs in the living-room. "But ye shouldnie speak ill o' the dead. And he's been dead a long time, puir man. Gallopin' consumption he had."

"I sometimes think that Eric's got consumption," Mrs. Laurie said. "He's been complaining of pains in his chest and head."

While his mother and Mrs. Watt were speaking, Eric lounged about. He never opened his mouth, but Mrs. Watt was acutely aware of his presence. He seemed to be getting continually in her road. She wished that he would go into another room or go outside, but he remained beside them. He did not appear to be listening to their conversation, but Mrs. Watt felt that nothing escaped him. She felt, too, that Mrs. Laurie would say much more if he were not there. All the time she watched her son, twisting her hands nervously.

Suddenly Eric spoke.

He said: "Is there any lemonade in the house?"

"No, dear," his mother said. "I don't think so, dear."

Eric said nothing. He stared in front of him, his lips drawn-in in a silent whistle.

"Did you want some lemonade, dear?" Mrs. Laurie said anxiously. "Take some money and go and get some, dear."

Eric lifted her bag from the sideboard and took out a two-shilling piece. He tossed it in the air and put it in his pocket. Mrs. Watt felt a sense of relief as he lounged out.

As soon as he had gone, Mrs. Laurie licked her lips nervously and said: "I really don't know what to do about Eric. He's not feeling well at all."

"Is it thae pains ye were tellin' me aboot?" said Mrs. Watt.

"Yes, I took him to a specialist and he examined him, but he didn't seem able to find anything wrong with him. I had to pay three guineas for the examination, and do you know what he said? You'll never guess, Mrs. Watt."

"I dinnie ken," Mrs. Watt said. "I never was ony guid at guessin'."

"He said——" Mrs. Laurie gulped. "He said: 'There's damn all wrong with him. You should get him a job.'"

Mrs. Watt tittered, but when she saw the look on Mrs. Laurie's face, she changed her titter into a cough and began to fill a pail at the sink.

"I'm terribly worried about him," Mrs. Laurie said. "I keep wondering whether I've done the right thing by him. Maybe I shouldn't have kept him at home like this. Maybe I've spoiled him. I don't know. But I felt that I needed company. After his father died, I simply had to have a man about the house."

"If ye'd been married to ma first joker you wouldnie think that," Mrs. Watt said, putting her pail on the scullery floor and flopping down beside it. "He was a lad——" wringing out her cloth and slapping it on the linoleum— "and a half! Never did an honest day's work in his life. He was aye sittin' in ma road. A fair scunner!"

Mrs. Laurie's fingers plucked nervously at the cords of her dressing-gown. "I wish I knew what to do about Eric," she said. "He'll have to register for the army next month."

"Ach, dinnie worry aboot that," Mrs. Watt said. "He doesnie look strong. They'll never take him."

"It's not that I was thinking about," Mrs. Laurie said. "I was wondering what I'd do if they didn't take him."

The front door banged, and Eric came in with three bottles of lemonade. He stared at his mother and Mrs. Watt, but there was no flicker of expression on his face. Mrs. Laurie stopped talking as soon as the door banged; she went away to her bedroom. Eric switched on the wireless and sat down beside it. He took three packets of chocolate from his pocket. Mrs. Watt eyed them, thinking to herself how she would thank him. But Eric began to eat the chocolate himself, never saying a word. Between bites he whistled tunelessly. After a while he opened one of the bottless and drank some of the lemonade. He nodded his head in time with the music from a jazz orchestra; his pale eyes staring at the window.

Mrs. Watt did some small jobs in the scullery. When she returned to the living-room she saw that Eric had opened another bottle and drank some of the lemonade, although he had drunk only a little out of the first bottle. She gave her head a puzzled shake and went to clean the bathroom.

She was wiping out the bath when Mrs. Laurie came in to speak to her. " How many days a week do you think you'll be able to come, Mrs. Watt?" she said in a low voice.

" How many days do you want me?" Mrs. Watt said.

" Well, I'd like you every day, but Eric says it's nonsense." Mrs. Laurie swallowed with embarrassment. " He says we don't really need a charwoman, and that he's quite capable of doing all the work himself. But, of course, I can't have him doing that." She looked uneasily behind her in the direction of the living-room. " Do you think you'd be able to come three days a week?"

" In the forenoons?" Mrs. Watt said. " I'd like away at twelve o'clock if possible."

" That'll be all right," Mrs. Laurie said. She lowered her voice again: " Don't say anything to Eric about how often you're going to come. He—er—well, he's never got on very well with any of the women we've had. But, of course, you're different," she added quickly. " He seems to be getting on all right with you."

" Ay," Mrs. Watt said.

" Just don't say anything to him," Mrs. Laurie said. " Nothing that'll make him angry. He's got an awful quick temper."

" All right," Mrs. Watt said.

She finished cleaning the bathroom, then she began to peel potatoes for the dinner. When she finished them, she went to ask Mrs. Laurie what else she would do. The bathroom door was half open, and Eric was busy cleaning the taps that Mrs. Watt had done already. He was whistling tunelessly, his eyes staring through the door at Mrs. Watt, staring straight through her.

" Never heed him," Mrs. Laurie whispered. " He's so used to cleaning everything himself that he thinks nobody else can do it. He won't even let me do it. Never mind him. It gives him something to do. We'll just have to humour him until he goes to the army."

Mrs. Watt was bewildered, but she said nothing; she kept looking anxiously at the clock. She wanted to get into the Cross Keys as soon as it opened; she needed a drink more badly to-day than she ever needed one. That laddie was just a bit more than she could bear. No wonder his mother looked as though she was being driven potty.

" Do you see that?" Mrs. Laurie cried.

Each of the bottles was open, and some lemonade had been taken out of each. The corks were lying on top of the wireless. Mrs. Laurie shook her head apologetically at Mrs. Watt and corked them. " Eric's so careless," she said. " I don't know how he'll do in the army. I wonder how he'll get on?"

" Oh, he'll get on all right," Mrs. Watt said.

But she wondered whether he would. She had an idea that the army would not deal with Eric as kindly and as softly as his mother had done. She did not know which of them she felt most sorry for.

Mrs. Laurie came to the door with her and whispered: " Now, you'll be sure to come back to-morrow?"

" Sure," Mrs. Watt said.

" That's a promise?" Mrs. Laurie said.

There was something so frightened and pathetic in her tone that Mrs. Watt could not say what she would have liked to say.

" Ay, that's a promise," she said.

But as she went down the path she wondered whether it was a promise she could keep. And when she turned at the gate and saw Eric staring at her out of the living-room window, she felt panic-stricken. She forced herself to smile, but there was no responding smile from him. He continued to stare straight in front of him. Just like a cat, Mrs. Watt thought, hurrying to reach the Cross Keys. Just like a cat waiting to pounce ... Or was it like a cat that had already pounced and was licking its lips after eating its prey?

14. PRIVATE WAR

The Johnsons had a private war in their air-raid shelter on the night that Edinburgh had its first air-raid. Ruby Johnson was preparing for bed when the sirens sounded at ten past twelve. She quickly pulled on the clothes she had just taken off, picked up her gas-mask and her handbag, and opened her bedroom door. From her parents' room she heard her mother crying: "Come on, hurry up!"

"Ach, I'm bidin' in ma bed." Pa Johnson's voice was grumpy and sleepy. "Ye're as safe in yer bed as anywhere else."

"Ye're gettin' up," Ma Johnson said. "And double quick about it! Ye ken fine what the wireless says about takin' cover. It's a farce to have an air-raid shelter and no' to take advantage o' it."

"I'm bidin' here," said Pa.

There was a sudden startled oath. Ruby grinned, realizing that her mother had pulled the bedclothes off him. "A' right," he grumbled. "I'll be there the now. Where's ma troosers?"

It was not very dark, and they could dimly see the people in the neighbouring gardens as they ran backwards and forwards between their houses and their shelters. They heard cries of "Bring the gas-masks!" and "Put out that light!"

Ruby helped her mother into their shelter, then she slid in after her. " Hell! " she said. " I've ripped my stocking."

" As long as that's all you get ripped, you'll not be bad," Ma Johnson said. " Where's that man?"

Ruby looked out of the shelter. " He's standing in the middle of the garden, looking up at the sky."

Her mother elbowed her aside and popped her head out of the opening. " Come inside at once, Pa! Standin' there like the lost sheep on the mountain! "

" Ach, I'll be there in a minute," he said. " I want to see all that's to be seen."

" Huh, he'll come in quick enough if he gets a bit shrapnel up his behind." Ma Johnson clicked her tongue with annoyance. " He thinks he'll be able to run after the bombs begin to fall."

" Well, they haven't started yet," Ruby said. " I don't hear anything. Do you?"

" Not even an aeroplane," Ma said. " Come inside, Pa," she called.

" Ach awa', woman, there's no danger yet. They're awa' up at the Forth Bridge. I see the searchlights up there."

" I dinnie care where they are," she cried. " You come inside at once."

But Pa continued to stand and gaze at the sky. " Eh, but I'd like to gi'e him a dad wi' a big stick," Ma said. " The aggravatin' auld devil."

" Gi'es a cigarette, Ruby," she said.

Ruby lit their cigarettes, then she cupped the match-flame in her hand and held it near her ankle, trying to see what damage had been done. " Put out that light in there! " her father cried. " The shelter's all lit up like a furnace. Do you want to show the Germans where we are? "

Ruby sniffed and settled back, trying to make herself as comfortable as she could on the wooden planks that had been rigged into a seat. Ma leaned her fat elbows on the ledge of the opening and leaned out. " You've awfu' little need to talk, Sidney Johnson," she said tartly. " The Germans couldnie find a better target than you. Will ye come inside when ye're tellt?"

" Ach, what are ye makin' a' the fuss aboot?" Pa said, sauntering over to the shelter. " There's time enough to come in when the shootin' starts. Ay, but it's a fine lookin' shelter," he said. "I'll have somethin' to say if they damage it."

"But no' as much as ye'd have to say if ye got damaged yersel'!" Ma Johnson laughed. "Come on inside."

"Will you come into my house said the spider to the fly!" Pa said as he climbed down into the shelter.

Ruby giggled. "I doubt you've got it wrong, Pa! It should be parlour."

"Funny kind o' parlour!" Ma sniffed. "I wouldnie like to sit in it long."

"Ach, we'll no' be here long," Pa said. "Everything's quiet. I doubt it's all over."

"Is it?" Ma said. "The calm before the storm!"

Pa was standing in the opening, peering up at the sky. "The searchlights are still lookin' for them," he said. "But I cannie see onythin'."

"Well, I wish they'd get them and let us get awa' back to oor beds," Ma said.

Pa began to dance up and down, singing: "Who'll come into ma wee hoose, ma wee hoose, ma wee hoose?"

"Shuttup," Ma said. "Or we'll no' be able to hear the bombs."

"Did ye ever see such an aggravatin' man?" she asked Ruby. "I wouldnie like to be ower often in an air-raid shelter wi' him. Standin' there in the door! I cannie see onythin' for him."

She shivered and drew her coat around her. "We'll be gettin' oor deaths o' cauld wi' them and their auld bombs."

"What aboot a wee nip?" Pa looked longingly in the direction of where he knew the small case was stored.

"No, no, that's for emergencies," Ma said.

"Well, this is an emergency, isn't it?"

"Ye're no' gettin' ony," Ma said. "Ye're a big enough handful when ye're sober. God knows what like ye'd be if ye were drunk."

"A wee thimbleful 'll do none o' us any harm," Pa said. "It'll keep out the cold."

"Ye're no' gettin' it," Ma said.

While her parents bickered, Ruby felt her ankle, trying to feel how much damage had been done. If only she could strike a match! She held her cigarette close to her leg, but although she bent down until her nose was almost scorched by the cigarette-end, she could see nothing. She wondered if she should risk going into the house and changing into another pair. She wouldn't like it if the house were bombed and she had to become a refugee wearing laddered stockings.

She looked out of the shelter. The searchlights were interlacing and occasionally meeting in a point in the centre of a large black mass of clouds. It was like a garish picture of a sun done in yellow chalk on a blackboard, only there was no huge ball of fire in the middle. The midnight sun, she thought, preparing to climb out.

"Where are ye goin', Ruby?"

"I'm just going into the house a minute for another pair of stockings."

"Ye're not goin' one foot." Ma puffed irritably at her cigarette, lighting the shelter dimly with the reflection. "Really, the idea! What if a bomb fell on the hoose when ye were in it? No, no, ye'll stay here."

"But I won't be a minute," Ruby said.

"Ye'll stay where ye are. D'ye hear me?" Ma said. "Really, I never saw such a pair o' aggravatin' folk."

"Ach, she'll be quite safe," Pa said. "No' that I can see what she wants to bother about another pair o' stockings for. Unless she wants to look nice when the A.R.P. wardens dig us oot o' the wreckage."

"Ye're a right comfort, Sidney Johnson," his wife said. "Who's talkin' about bein' dug out o' the wreckage? I wouldnie like to trust masel' to our Air-Raid wardens, onyway. Like enough they're a' sittin' safe in their own shelters. I wouldnie lippen on them helpin' us."

Ruby sighed and sat down again. A quarter of an hour passed slowly. There was a sound of planes faintly in the distance for a short time, then silence. Another quarter of an hour passed. Ruby held her cigarette close to the face of her watch every few minutes. She yawned and shivered with the cold. She wished that she had brought a cushion with her. "We'll have to mind and bring cushions the next time," she said.

"Ay, if there is a next time," Ma said.

"Ach, I think we should get awa' back to oor beds," Pa said wearily. "I doubt all the excitement's over."

"Ye're not goin' one foot," Ma said. "Not till the All-Clear goes."

"Maybe it'll no' go," Pa said. "I doubt they've forgotten about it. We could be sittin' here a' night for a' they care. How long ha'e we been here, Ruby?"

"An hour."

"Ach, I'm awa' back to ma bed."

"Just you dare!" Ma said. "Just you dare!"

Pa sat back with a muttered oath. Another half an hour passed, and every few minutes he grumbled and spoke about returning to his bed. Ruby yawned and wished they would both be quiet. Her hand went continually to her ankle. At last Mrs. Johnson began to say that maybe they had better go back to bed. "Maybe the All-Clear's gone and we havenie heard it," she said. "I wouldnie be surprised; yer father was makin' that much noise!"

Just then there were three loud reports and a burst of machine-gun firing. "Gosh, that's near enough!" Pa said, hurrying to the mouth of the shelter and poking out his head.

"Keep in, keep in, ye daft auld devil!" Ma caught his jacket and tugged it. "Come on in or ye'll get hit!"

But Pa remained at the mouth of the shelter, gazing up at the sky. "There it is!" he cried. "There it is!"

Ma gave a tremendous heave and succeeded in pulling him in. As she did so there was another burst of firing. "Ach, to damn, I've missed it!" Pa cried. "What did ye want to do that for? They were just pickin' him out wi' the search-lights. And now ye've made me miss it! I could ha'e seen the whole thing if it hadnie been for you."

Ruby yawned, thinking that no matter how much noise there was outside, she couldn't have heard anything for the noise her parents were making. Her yawn twisted into a smile. It was just like the British to go out fighting. Even though it was with each other!

"Listen!" Ma cried. "Listen!"

"Oh, thank goodness!" she said. "There's the All Clear at last!"

In a few minutes they were all safely back in the house. "I'll make a cup o' tea," Ma said. "We'll need somethin' after that."

"Ay, a wee nip," Pa said. But his wife gave him a look and put on the kettle.

"I don't want any tea, thanks," Ruby said. "I think I'll away to my bed." She yawned. "Good night."

They called good night as she climbed the stair. She peeled her clothes off sleepily, and sat down on the edge of the bed. Over two hours of sitting in a cold shelter was something that she didn't want to happen every night. She was preparing to swing her legs into the bed when she remembered something. Oh, I'll do it in the morning, she thought. But she thrust the thought aside. Better do it now. Sighing wearily, she yawned and opened a drawer in her dressing-chest. She was so sleepy that she could scarcely see what she was doing. Ah, here they were! She took out a pair of stockings and put them in her handbag. And she smiled as she got into bed. She was completely prepared now for the next air-raid!

15. BACKGREEN CONCERT

Mrs. Logan treadled with determination. "I'll see that Phyllis knocks spots off thae other bairns," she said to Mrs. Stout, her friend from the bottom flat, who was sitting on the edge of the table. "She's goin' to be the star o' this concert or I'll know the reason why!" She punched in the last few stitches and pulled out the frock, holding it up and shaking it with a flourish: a pale blue flag of mother's pride.

"It's gorgeous," Mrs. Stout said, pitching her cigarette-end into the fire before she fingered the dress. "Phyllis'll look gorgeous in it."

"I'd like to see that Mrs. Benzies's face when she sees it," Mrs. Logan said. "Her bandy-legged brat'll no' have a look in."

Mrs. Stout sighed. "I wish it was for a brat o' mine. Jock was just sayin' last night that he wished we had a bairn in the concert."

"Ach, there's time enough yet," Mrs. Logan said. "Ye've only been married five years. Ye'll just have to keep hopin'. And mind the motto: Try, try, try again!"

"It would be fine if the Goldengreen Street concert was better than ony o' the other Calderburn ones," Mrs. Stout said. "I see in the *News* last night that Calderburn Crescent had sent fifty-five shillings to the Red Cross fund."

"Ach, we'll make mair than that," Mrs. Logan said. "That was just a flea-bite."

"I made a lot o' tablet," Mrs. Stout said. "I thought I'd ha'e to do somethin' seein' that I hadnie ony bairns o' ma ain in it. Cissie McIntosh said she'd sell it at the concert. It should maybe rake in some money."

"I hear that wife Benzies gave a basket o' groceries for the bairns to raffle," said Mrs. Logan, spreading an ironing-blanket on the table. "She should raffle hersel' when she's at it. Though she wouldnie bring in much wi' yon horse's face!"

"I was speakin' to her last night when she was doin' the passage," Mrs. Stout said, putting the cover on the sewing-machine and gathering up the clippings of blue silk. "She tells me that her and Mrs. Rafferty are goin' to do a dance at the concert."

"What!" cried Mrs. Logan. "I thought it was just to be the bairns."

"Well, that's what she told me."

"Huh, they'll be a couple o' bonnie dearies, and I never saw them," Mrs. Logan said. "Honest to God, I never heard the like o' it. Twa big women goin' to dance in a kids' concert."

"Maybe Rafferty's tryin' to make up for that laddie o' hers. He's no' to be in it, is he?"

"I should think not! He's that daft that he couldnie be trusted to do the right thing at the right time. Honest to God," Mrs. Logan said, "I never saw such a daft bairn. He goes on like a mad one, aye playin' cowboys and Indians and pretendin' he's shootin' folk. Shootin' himsel' and lyin' doon in the middle o' the street for 'oors. He'll get a bonnie fright one o' thae days if a motor gangs ower him."

"It's a pity a motor wouldnie gang ower his mother. That woman causes more rows in this street than onybody else." Mrs. Stout leaned forward, her eyes big with spite. "Did ye hear aboot her throwin' a pail o' water ower Mrs. Moore?"

"Ay, I heard." Mrs. Logan began to iron the frock, smoothing out the frills with great care. "She had a right neck. Mrs. Moore just said what was the truth, about

Rafferty havin' a bairn by some engine-driver before she married Rafferty."

"Really!" Mrs. Stout exclaimed. "A woman like that has a right cheek to dance for the Red Cross."

"Well, we'll see," Mrs. Logan said, smiling as the iron slid smoothly over the silk. "We'll just wait and see."

The concert was held on the drying-green between two tenements. Almost everybody in the street had loaned chairs or seats of some description, and these were arranged in a semi-circle around a stage composed of tables and boards. Mrs. Logan and Mrs. Stout were early, and Mrs. Logan said: "We'll be able to bag good seats!"

"I'll have this auld easy-chair," said Mrs. Stout. "Here, shift that yin beside it."

"The grand stand!" Mrs. Logan laughed as she pulled the two big chairs together. "Now, we're all set!"

Apparently some people were not going to come down and sit in the improvised theatre; they leaned out of their windows. "Hey, you up there in the gallery," Mrs. Logan called to one stout woman whose bosom was overhanging her elbows. "Mind and gi'e the man at the door yer tickets!"

"Tryin' to get a free show," she muttered to her friend. "Although there's to be a collection, just catch the like o' her throwin' oot ony money. She's a right skinflint."

"Who's that?" Mrs. Stout asked, nodding at some women who were taking their seats. "That one wi' the red tammy."

"Oh, that's wee pug-nose that the bomb fell on," Mrs. Logan said, waving to some people who were arranging themselves at a top-storey window. "Ye ken—Mrs. something or other—Flockart—frae Calderburn Gardens. Ye mind, the incendiary bomb fell on her hoose last week."

"I hope there'll no' be an air-raid while the concert's on," said Mrs. Stout.

"Oh well, if there is we're fine and near the shelters." Mrs. Logan nodded to the seats arranged on top of the Anderson shelters. "We'll just ha'e to make a dive into auld Nicholson's dug-out."

"No' me, I'm no' goin' into it." Mrs. Stout sniffed and shook back her short permanently-waved hair. "He wasnie very pleasant to the McIntoshes when they went into his shelter in the raid last Thursday because their own was flooded."

"Ach, he's a right auld nark. Did ye ever see the like o' that?" Mrs. Logan nodded at the fence that Mr. Nicholson had put up around his vegetables. "Fancy puttin' big palin' stabs like that. Ye'd think it was for keepin' an elephant in!"

"Maybe it's for his auld woman!" Mrs. Stout giggled. "She looks as though she should be shut up."

"It's strong enough to keep twa ponies in, onyway." Mrs. Logan leaned past her and said; "How are ye the night, Mrs. Moore? Have ye got ower the fright ye got the other night?"

"Ay, I'm fine." Fat Mrs. Moore lowered herself into the chair next to Mrs. Stout. "I hear that Her Nabs is goin' to do a dance."

"Ay. Have ye brought a pail o' water wi' ye?"

"No, but it would be a grand chance!" Mrs. Moore's fat shoulders shook with laughter.

A little girl selling tablet squeezed her way towards them. "How're ye gettin' on, Cissie?" asked Mrs. Stout. "Is it sellin' all right?"

"Uhuh. I've sellt mair than half o' it already."

"That's fine." Mrs. Stout took out her purse. "We'll take a couple o' bars to help ye on."

She handed one of the bars to Mrs. Logan. "It tastes no' bad though I say it masel'." She was leaning back with satisfaction, nibbling the tablet, when Mrs. Logan nudged her and said: "There's yer man ower there. He looks as though he's wantin' ye."

A youngish man with a bald head and shaving-soap on his face was leaning on a fence, trying to attract Mrs. Stout's attention. He was in his shirt-sleeves, and his shirt was tucked down below his breast so that the hair on his chest could be seen. "What do ye want, Jock?" his wife cried.

He waved to her to come to him. She opened her mouth wide with exasperation and began to scramble through the chairs, apologizing to the people she disturbed. Mrs. Moore winked at Mrs. Logan. "Thae young ones!" she said. "Their wives cannie get the length o' the lavvies wi'oot them followin'!"

"I never thought he was such a queer lookin' jeeger," a woman said. "I've never seen him wi'oot his hat afore. He's just like a bald skatin' rink."

"His breast was bare, his matted hair!" Mrs. Moore laughed. "As ma man that's aye spoutin' poetry would say!"

"Wheesht!" a woman cried. "The concert's goin' to start!"

A young woman with a piano-accordion at the side began to play a popular tune, and all the little girls of the street filed on to the improvised stage, giggling self-consciously and pushing each other. One or two of them tried to do the step they had been taught, but most of them were so busy looking for their mothers and friends that they could do nothing. Mrs. Logan twiddled her thumbs and tucked in her chin with pride. Although she said it herself, Phyllis was far and away the best dressed and the neatest of the bunch. Just look at that bairn, Maisie Benzies, now! Her mother's frizzed out the poor bairn's hair until it looks like a heather-besom. "Did ye ever see the like o' it?" she whispered to Mrs. Stout, who had pushed her way back to her seat, her face scarlet with embarrassment. "It's just like something that comes out a Ewbank!"

"Do ye ken what Jock wanted?" Mrs. Stout murmured.

Mrs. Logan gave her a dunch. "Be quiet the now. Phyllis is goin' to dance."

Phyllis, gripping the frills of her frock with both hands, her little fingers sticking out with priggish elegance, had minced to the front of the stage. She bowed left and right, and nodded to the girl with the accordion.

Mrs. Logan sat back and watched every step, nodding her head every now and then in time with her daughter's feet. "There now," she muttered. "One, two, one, two, turn. . . ."

She simpered and ostentatiously folded her arms when the crowd applauded at the end of her daughter's dance. "She was gorgeous," said Mrs. Stout, and when Mrs. Moore leaned over and said: "I couldnie ha'e done better masel'!" Mrs. Logan smiled with satisfaction.

The next turn was Mrs. Benzies and Mrs. Rafferty. They shook their fists and roared remarks to the audience when they came on. Mrs. Rafferty had on her husband's sailor clothes, his hat tilted to the side of her dark curly hair, and she wore a pair of high-heeled red quilted satin bedroom slippers. Mrs. Benzies had on a frilly ballet-dress, which she flirted up every little while, showing her lace-trimmed yellow cami-knickers. The audience hooted and applauded its approval of this comic by-play.

"There's Rafferty himsel'," Mrs. Logan said, jerking her head to the crowd standing on the outskirts. "He's got on his civvies. By God, he'd get a fright if a captain or somebody off his boat came and found his wife wearin' his navy clothes!"

"They're a pair o' comics, aren't they?" the woman next to Mrs. Logan said, clapping her hands loudly and laughing when the two women had finished their dance.

"I daresay it pleases some folk," Mrs. Logan replied, giving her palms one or two feeble claps together. "But it's no' to everybody's taste."

But it was to the audience's taste if it wasn't to Mrs. Logan's; they demanded an encore. Mrs. Rafferty came to the front and bawled: "We're ower winded to dance again the noo, but we'll ha'e a song. Come on, noo! *Roll Out the Barrel!* We'll roll it right ower auld Hitler's belly!"

There were shrieks of laughter and when the accordion struck up the tune they shouted the words of the song lustily. But Mrs. Logan sat through it with a disapproving face. This was a concert that the bairns had arranged, and she didn't see why those two besoms should have come and stuck their noses into it, even though Mrs. Starke and the rest thought they were so comic. If they were so keen, they could do their bit in other ways and leave the bairns alone to do theirs.

Mrs. Rafferty and Mrs. Benzies danced again towards the end of the concert, and again they led the crowd in community singing. Mrs. Logan was so furious that she could not join in singing her favourite song: *I have not got my specs with me.* But she brightened a little when Phyllis did another dance, and when the concert finished she said goodnight amicably enough to the others. After all, she thought, Phyllis was easy the star among the bairns. That brat o' Benzies' was just a mess.

It was beginning to get dark; the tenements were standing like stiff cardboard boxes against a beryl sky, which was striped with thin flame-coloured clouds. Wispy slate-blue clouds were puffing upwards in the light of the fading sun. A crowd of men and boys were taking down the improvised stage and carrying chairs back to their owners. Mrs. Logan looked at the sky. " Let's hope there's no raids the night," she said as they went into the entry and began to climb the stairs. She put her arm proudly and protectingly around her daughter's shoulders. " Ye knocked spots off everybody there, Phyllis. Though it's masel' that says it! "

16. DIRTY MINNIE

Dirty Minnie said she had been going to wash her feet when Winnie the Wailer went. "I wasnie wantin' to wash them, mind ye," she said to the other women in the shelter, "but they were that sair that I thought I'd gi'e them a bit steep in hot water. I was just tryin' to pluck up strength to take the kettle offen the fire when the sireen blew, so I said, Ach to hell, I'll wash them the morn!"

"Ay, if ye're still alive to tell the tale," the woman in the corner said dolorously.

"Ach you!" Dirty Minnie laughed. "Ye're aye lookin' for snaw afore it comes on! Here, tak' a wee sup o' stout. That'll cheer ye up a bit."

She peered over her enormous bust and fished in her message-bag, taking out two bottles of stout and a crumpled five of Woodbines. "This is a' I had time to bring wi' me," she said. "I just planked them in ma bag, put ma shawl ower ma head and dived doon the stair."

"Like a paper-ship in full sail!" laughed Mrs. Ryan. "I met her in the entry, breezin' along. At first I thocht it was a bomb, then I saw it was Minnie. She seemed a' bust and a' belly!"

"Ye're jealous!" Minnie grinned, and uncorked one of the bottles. "Ye're that wee and skinny, folk would never tak' ye for onythin' else but yer auld man's pipecleaner!"

" Mind and no' spill that stout on ma clean boards," the woman in the corner said sharply. " I scrubbed them a' wi' lysol this mornin', and I'm no' wantin' them a' mucked up!"

" Tae hell wi' you and yer auld boards!" said Minnie cheerfully. " Ye'd think this shelter was a palace the way ye're aye scrubbin' and cleanin' at it. Shakin' oot the rugs every day and airin' the mattresses. It's a wonder ye dinnie bother to put fresh floo'ers in the jam-jar!"

" Ay, it's easy seen that ye have nothin' better to dae, Mrs. Milligan," said Mrs. Ryan, reaching out for the cup of stout that Minnie handed to her. " If ye had twa or three bairns ye wouldnie bother aboot cleanin' oot the shelter."

" Ay, or a lodger or twa!" Minnie held up her cracked cup and said: " Here's tae us a' and tae hell wi' Hitler!" before gulping down her stout.

Mrs. Milligan sniffed and said: " Well, yer lodgers dinnie seem to get that much o' yer attention, Minnie. Ony time I see ye ye're either oot gallivantin' or hangin' oot the window."

" Och, ma lodgers dinnie mind," Minnie said. " They just tak' me the way I am!"

" Sailors don't care!" Mrs. Ryan said, taking the cigarette Minnie held out.

" Was that an airyplane I heard?" Mrs. Milligan cried, cocking her shrewish face to the side.

" No, it was just ma belly rumblin'!" Minnie laughed, and struck a match. " Ye're aye hearin' airyplanes! Ye're like Joe, yin o' ma sailors; he's aye hearin' submarines!"

" Well, he'll no' hear many submarines at the docks doon at Petersfield," Mrs. Milligan said sarcastically. " Dry land sailors! They've got a grand cushy job."

" They're no' dry-land sailors at a'," Minnie said. " They've got a right dangerous job playin' aboot wi' a' thae mines. It's a' their chance if they can get into a comfortable bed every second nicht."

" Ay, if it is a comfortable bed!" said Mrs. Milligan.

Minnie blew a mouthful of cigarette-smoke towards the sand-bags at the opening of the shelter, and putting her hands on her fat thighs she leaned forward. " Listen here, is it a fight ye're lookin' for? Because if it is I'll paste the lights oot o' ye!"

"I never said onythin' oot o' place, did I?" Mrs. Milligan began to look scared. It was all very well baiting Dirty Minnie, but when she got that threatening look on her face it was time to call a halt.

"Well, just you leave ma beds alone," Minnie said, relaxing again into her usual comfortable easy-oseyness. "Ma sailors have nothin' against them. They're damned glad to come up to ma hoose every second nicht and get a decent sleep after the bunks they ha'e on that wee cramped boat."

"And I'm damned glad to ha'e them!" She laughed. "I dinnie ken what I'd dae wi'oot them. They keep me supplied wi' a' the tea and meat and fags and stuff that I want. I never need to ken that there's a war on."

"Ye're lucky," Mrs. Milligan said, glad to see that the danger signal was past. "I wish I could get some lodgers like them. I've had dozens in my time, but never one that stayed longer than a week or twa. I'm sure I did ma best for them, cleanin' and seein' that their beds were comfortable and that they got their meals on time. But they never stopped for mair than a week or twa. They aye had some excuse. Ardingtown was ower far awa' frae the centre o' Glesca or somethin'. They didnie like the neebors or they had ower far to go to their work. Yon last yin I had, Mr. Veitch. My God, I'll never forget what he said. The impiddent brute. I was glad to get rid o' him. He said: 'The people here come from the slums and they're makin' Ardingtown back into a slum as quick as they can.'"

Dirty Minnie laughed and drank off her stout, but the rest of the women began to speak indignantly about the uppishness of the unlamented Mr. Veitch. They were still airing their views when the All Clear sounded. Minnie picked up her bag and stuffed the empty bottles into it. "Well, I'd better get awa' up and get ma lads' tea ready for them," she said, pushing her way out of the shelter. "Or they'll be here afore I can cough."

"Dae ye never think what would happen to ye if yer lodgers' boat got blown up by a mine?" Mrs. Ryan said as they went into the entry.

"Och ay, I often think aboot it," Minnie said. "But och to pot, what's the guid o' thinkin' aboot things like that. It just turns yer hair grey, and mine's grey enough already!"

She stood and spoke to Mrs. Ryan for a while, then she stopped outside her door to have a few words with Mrs. McIntosh. She had just got in, and was putting on the kettle when the three sailors came in. "Ay there, Minnie the Moocher!" Joe cried, slapping her bottom as he passed her on his way to the sink. "She was a great big hoochy-coocher!"

"G'out ye nasty brute!" Minnie grinned.

George flung his sailor's hat on to a chair, put a parcel on the table and began to rake inside his blouse. "That's your steak, Minnie. And here's your fags. I had a terrible job gettin' them from the Old Man. He raised blue hell. He was playin' Nap and he didn't want to be bothered goin' to the safe for them."

"The lazy auld devil," Minnie said. "Hoo does he think folk are goin' to live if they dinnie get their fags?" She un-wrapped the parcel and sniffed the meat. "This is real fine steak. Better than the stuff ye buy in the butcher's. I dinnie ken what I'd dae if it wasnie for you laddies."

"We don't know what we'd do without you, Minnie!" George laughed. "You give us a home from home!"

"Home was never like this!" Toots said, settling himself in a chair by the fire and stretching out his legs over the cinder-covered hearth. "What have you been doin' to-day, Minnie?"

"Just muckin' aboot," Minnie said, slapping the steak into the frying-pan.

"You're tellin' us!" George said, looking around and winking at the others. "You lazy old devil, you! You've never even swept up the shavings that Joe made on Tuesday night when he mended the table."

"Och to pot!" Minnie said. "Sweep them up yersel' if ye're no' pleased." She gave the fryingpan a shake before turning over the steak. "Here, Toots, if ye're wantin' ony tea ye'd better set the table."

Immediately the three young men began to get in each other's way, laying cups and saucers and plates of different shapes and patterns on the soiled crumby tablecloth. They jostled each other good-naturedly on their way to and from the cupboard. Joe still wore his sailor's hat cocked over his forehead. George kept sticking his chewing-gum on to his front teeth and sucking it off noisily.

"Oh, Minnie was a slave-driver!" Toots sang, banging two plates together like cymbals. "But Minnie had a heart as big as a whale . . ."

They put their arms around each others' shoulders and tried to harmonize:

"As big as a whale!"

" AS BIG AS A WHALE!"

"Oh, Minnie was as dirty as a tanker, but she had a heart bigger than a banker!"

"G'out ye daft devils!" Minnie brought the frying-pan over to the table. "Haud yer tongues and haud oot yer plates!"

"Gosh, but the Old Man was in a right rage the night," George said, chewing his first mouthful. "Him and the Chief and yon P.O. with the pawly arm were playin' Nap when I went in to get the cigarettes, and the Old Man didn't want to bother his backside gettin' them for me. You'll get them to-morrow, he says. To-morrow, I says, but what good'll they be to me to-morrow? I want them to-day. Well, you can't get them to-day, he says. But we're supposed to get them to-day, I says. You know the rule. Twenty cigarettes, duty free, to each man every day. See? But the old mucker didn't want to bother his ass. What do you want them for, anyway? he says. You don't smoke. I know I don't smoke, I says. But the rest of the boys do. I always give my share of cigarettes to them. Ask any of them and they'll tell you. Jesus, but he was in a flamin' row at havin' to leave his Nap and go to the safe for them. I'll watch you for this, George, he says. The old bastard. I'll watch him. If he knew the things I could pin on him. Gettin' meat from the store and sellin' it. And sellin' cigarettes and tobacco on the pier. *Our* cigarettes and tobacco! Jesus, the graft that goes on down at those docks. The Old Man's only one that's makin' a pile. All those bloody P.O.s are pilin' in money hands down. It's a great war for some of them. Jesus, it would make you sick."

" Come on and finish yer steak afore it gets cauld," Minnie said kindly. "Dinnie bother aboot what happens doon at the docks."

"Well, I can't help it," George said. "It fair makes my blood boil. All that graft."

"Aw, why worry?" Joe said. "Maybe you won't have to worry about it much longer."

The sailors were silent. They chewed their meat, swilling it down with strong tea. None of them looked at Minnie. They scowled at the grease-spots on the table-cloth.

"Er—Minnie . . ."

"Ay, Joe, what's wrong wi' ye noo?" Minnie leaned back and picked her teeth with a hair-pin, sucking away the scraps of meat that the pin loosened.

"We're maybe goin' away," Joe said. "Got the news to-day. Word of the boat bein' shifted to another base. Maybe Aberdeen or Hull."

Minnie went on picking her teeth. Nobody looked at anybody else. "We don't want to go, Minnie," Toots said gloomily. "We're fine and comfortable here."

"Anybody want mair tea?" Minnie said, reaching for the pot.

"Ah well," Minnie said after a while. "If ye have to go we cannie help it. It's the way of the world. But ye're no' shifted yet. There's time enough to worry aboot snaw when it comes on."

She put the hair-pin back in her greasy bun and rose from the table. "What aboot goin' to the picters? There's a guid ,yin in the Embassy. Gene Autry and Smiley Burnette. It should be guid."

"Okay," Joe said. "Maybe we're not goin' away at all, mind. Only there's word about it. We just thought we'd better tell you in time."

"Well, ye're no' awa' yet," Minnie said. "But it's high time we were gettin' awa' to the picters if we're goin' to get in. Come on, hurry and get yer skates on! We'll leave the dishes till the morn."